Mistletoe Mishap

Amish Bachelors Christmas: Book 1

Copyright © 2020 by Samantha Bayarr

All rights reserved. No part of this book may be reproduced in any form, either written or electronically, without the express permission from the author.

This novel is a work of fiction. Names, characters, and incidents are the product of the author's imagination and are therefore used fictitiously. Any similarity or resemblance to actual persons, living or dead, places, or events is purely coincidental and beyond the intent of the author or publisher.

Amish Bachelors Christmas:

Mistletoe Mishap

Sometimes, you just have to go with your gut instinct!

TABLE OF CONTENTS

CHAPTER ONE

CHAPTER TWO

CHAPTER THREE

CHAPTER FOUR

CHAPTER FIVE

CHAPTER SIX

CHAPTER SEVEN

CHAPTER EIGHT

CHAPTER NINE

CHAPTER TEN

EPILOGUE

Mistletoe Mishap

CHAPTER ONE

"What do you mean, you *promised* me to Cousin Silas?"

Holly Yoder punched a hole in the bread dough and plucked it from the large mixing bowl, smacking it down on the prep table with a thud. She pushed her fist into it, pursing her lips. Taking out her frustrations on bread dough was a first for her, but it was better than sassing her father.

Bread dough stuck to her fingers, adding to her frustration. She grabbed the scoop from the flour bin and spread it over the lump of half-kneaded bread dough in front of her, sending a cloud of flour dust all over the kitchen. Leaning against the prep table to brace her wobbly legs, she glared at her father and waited for him to explain.

Her father lowered his gaze. "I'm ashamed to admit that after we sold our *haus* in Grabill, we didn't have enough money to move to this community. So, I borrowed about five thousand dollars from Cousin Henry to pay the difference."

"*Dat,* why?" she asked, tears welling up in her throat.

She continued to knead the dough with an anger that could not be quenched no matter how many times she pushed and pulled at it.

"It was the only way we could buy the bakery," he said with a gentle tone.

As if his tone made a difference to her right now.

"After that hailstorm wiped out my crops, we wouldn't have made it through the winter if I hadn't sold the *haus* and the land," he continued. "Besides, I'm getting too old to work on a farm. I needed a change, and your cousins offered to help."

"And now you're indebted to them," she fumed. "*I'm* indebted to them for it."

Her father shook his head. "It sounds so much worse when you say it that way."

"How much worse can it get to be promised to marry your third cousin? A *mann* I don't even know."

"You met him a time or two when you were younger," her father said.

"I don't remember him, and I don't love him!" she cried. "How embarrassing it is that *mei dat* sold me like a horse or a cow!"

She hadn't even had the chance to make any friends in their new community. How friendly would the women be when they found out her father matched her with her own cousin? They would look upon her with pity instead of friendship, and she would have a tough time facing her own reflection without thinking the same thing.

"You've been wanting to get married, and you were never going to get the chance to do that by helping me work that broken-down farm and taking care of me for the rest of your life," he said.

She wanted very much to get married, but not to Silas—even if he was her third cousin.

What's wrong?" her father asked. "All you've talked about for the past year is getting married. I thought I was doing something to help you along."

She sniffed back tears and pushed at the bread dough once more. "I changed my mind; I'm not ready to get married."

It was a lie that forced her to lift up a prayer to her heavenly father asking for forgiveness, but she just couldn't stand by and let her father marry her off to a man she didn't love.

"This way, I can take care of you with the profits from the bakery, and neither of us has to break our backs out in the field anymore," the man continued. "You'll have a husband and won't have to work so hard; you can work the bakery with me, and we'll both be happier."

You mean you'll be happier!

She punched at the dough again, not feeling the emotional release she sought. "I agreed to sell the *haus* and get this bakery with you because I thought it would be easier for you after the bad break we had with the crops," she said. "But that was *before* I knew that you promised me to be married without even asking me. You made me part of a business deal, and you've shamed me."

Her father creased his brow at her statement. "You have a bakery to inherit now instead of a broken-down farm, and the loft makes a nice roof over your head."

"We have been here for two weeks already," Holly said. "Why have you waited until now to tell me this?"

"Because I was afraid you would stay in Grabill with your cousins and not come here with me," he said. "I believe *Gott* has many blessings for us here."

"Like me getting married to my cousin, Silas?" she groused. "I can still go back to Grabill, *Dat!*"

"It's too late for that," he said. "I already took the money and used it to pay the remainder of the bakery expenses. I asked Henry for a little time to break the news to you, but Silas won't wait any longer; he wants to begin courting you right away so you can marry before Christmas."

"But Christmas is only three weeks away!" she cried.

"That's why he's insisting the two of you start to get reacquainted," her father said.

"But I don't want to marry him, *Dat*," she cried.

Her father looked at her thoughtfully. "Will you make me a promise?'

"What's that?"

"Go for a buggy ride with him and see how it goes," he suggested. "Give it a try; if you can't do it, I'll find a way to pay Cousin Henry."

"*Dat*, you know you won't make a profit from this place so soon!"

"Then I suggest we pray hard for a miracle," he said with a sad smile.

Holly knew he could never come up with that kind of money, and that's why he agreed to the arrangement in the first place. He was a prideful man who would not accept a loan, but making a barter was more to his suiting. If she had any chance at all of getting out this arrangement, she would have to take matters into her own hands.

"I didn't mean to hurt my only *dochder,*" her father continued. "But I know your *mudder* would have wanted you to be married and have a *familye* by now—not still helping me and breaking our backs with that farm."

The mere mention of her mother stirred a sadness in her that she was determined to leave behind in Grabill. She'd made a promise to her mother that she would find a good man and fall in love—not marry her cousin—a man she could never love.

She sighed. This would be their second Christmas without her, and Holly suspected part of her father's decision to pick up and move was so he wouldn't have to face another Christmas in that house full of memories of her mother. She knew her father hadn't asked for the hailstorm that had ruined their corn crop, but she was certain he'd been praying for a way to leave the house and the community.

She supposed God had provided a way to get them out for sure because she knew her father probably wouldn't have left otherwise. She'd hated to see him so sad and miserable, but worried he was running from his grief instead of facing it. She believed God had given them a new start, but she could not believe God would have her marry a man she didn't love—unless it was a test of her love for her earthly father. Surely, she could do this for him, couldn't she?

Holly shook off the bad feeling she had about the whole thing and went back to work on making the bread for the day. Right now, all she really wanted was to feel the icy December wind against her cheeks as she skated as fast as she could around the pond behind their house back in Grabill. But that wasn't going to get her anywhere; all she could do was to pray for a miracle to get her out of having to marry Silas.

Benjamin Bontrager pulled up his collar to shield the wind as he hitched his horse to the family buggy. He needed to get into town for supplies for his mother before the snow got any deeper, and driving the buggy would be too much of a chore.

Christmas was only three weeks away, and already, they'd had so much snow this year, he'd barely had a chance to take care of much apart from the tree farm and the sales lot in town. But since the county snowplow had finally made its way down their country road late this morning, he knew it was time to venture past the Bishop's house where his brother, Luke, had pulled the sleigh to take them to church yesterday. The *Englishers* had made their way to their tree farm already this morning with no trouble since some of them still enjoyed cutting their own trees, but the snow on the roads had been too deep for their horse to drag the buggy through. Even now, there was only one narrow pass, but he appreciated it anyway.

He and his brothers had been cooped up quite a bit this winter with the accumulation of snow, and Ben was tired of having nothing but them for company. Their only respite had been driving the sleigh into town to run the tree lot, and even then, they'd drawn straws to see who could go and who would stay behind to take care of the customers at the farm.

It made for a lonelier winter than past years when he and his brothers had attended many of the Sunday night singings. They hadn't been to a singing since the harvest, and that had made the cold winter seem longer. Even though this was their busiest time of the year, selling Christmas trees to the *Englishers* did not keep him from feeling lonely for the company of a pretty woman.

Ben was growing up fast and wanted a family of his own. He loved taking care of his immediate family, but it was not getting him any closer to that particular dream. After Hannah passed him up for another man, he'd given up hope of finding a woman to marry, until Sunday when he'd met the new family in their community who just happened to have a daughter his age—his and Luke's, but his twin wasn't interested in her.

Ben was very interested; he wanted more out of his life than Christmas trees and *Englishers'* money. He loved the pine trees; he loved the smell of them, but they'd become a bit of a chore that was making him feel old before his time.

Today, he planned to stop by the bakery downtown to get some fresh-baked bread and some sweets since his mother had fallen behind in her kitchen work after she sprained her ankle. The doctor had told her to stay off it as much as possible, which meant they would have no bread for a couple of weeks. It would be a nice treat for her to have a break from baking, but Ben and his brothers would also welcome the warm treats from the bakery that they'd been missing the past few days.

Ben had another reason for going to the bakery; his interest in seeing a certain young woman who worked there.

She and her father were new to the community, and they'd reopened the downtown bakery almost two weeks ago. Ben had only just learned of their move yesterday at the service. He had spent the entire meal afterward trying to get up the nerve to talk to her, but aside from a few smiling glances across the room, she hadn't left her father's side the entire day. His decision to visit the bakery was so he could talk to her without her father, church members, or his brothers hovering too close-by.

The lovely young woman had sat across from him during church services on Sunday, but she'd never even looked his way, though he'd been completely distracted by her the entire service. He'd been talking to his brother when the Bishop first introduced them, so he hadn't caught the young woman's name. When he finally looked up and made eye-contact with her, he'd become so enamored with her dark green eyes that reminded him of holly leaves and her auburn hair with a tint of red in it, that he could hardly sit still. Luke had scolded him, claiming that he'd been better-behaved during Sunday service when he was a toddler.

His brother was too busy acting like their father to notice the pretty woman even if she came right up to him and kicked him.

Luke had taken over as head of the family a few years back after their father had passed away, and he sometimes acted a lot older than the seven minutes that separated them in age. As his older, fraternal twin, Luke had never let him live it down that he was the oldest. Because of that, he'd spent most of his life growing up too fast trying to prove it. He didn't have time for romance and courting, and would scold Ben if he knew what he was up to now.

Luke had been taking care of their father's role in the family for so long, he'd forgotten what it was like to be young and wanting to court. Ben had recently become a little more anxious since, other than Luke, most of his peers were already married. He was tired of being a bachelor.

Ben fully intended to help care for his ailing mother even once he got married, but he was never going to get that chance. They were always so busy with the Christmas trees this time of the year, and four wedding seasons had passed him by already.

Today, Ben decided he was going to take his future into his own hands. It was now or never; if he didn't secure a wife for himself this year, he'd be too old by next season. He'd get lumped in with the widowers as far as chances for marrying went. He'd warned

Luke to start looking too, and he felt rather selfish going after the new girl in town who didn't seem to have any sisters for his brothers.

Feeling desperate, Ben knew that if he didn't get to her first, he might miss his chance. Sure, she was probably more Simon's age, but his younger brother was too much like Luke to pay the woman any mind. With Jonas out on *rumspringa,* that left Ben to pursue her himself.

When he finally reached downtown, he was so jittery he could hardly think straight. But he had to remind himself that he had a reason to be at the bakery where the beautiful young woman worked, and he hoped he wouldn't trip over himself trying to put in an order for his mother.

Ben leaned over in the buggy seat and rested his elbows on his knees as he steered the buggy toward the bakery. Snowflakes drifted lazily from the clouds while the sun tried to peek out from between them.

Would she know that he was Amish, or would she think he was Mennonite by how he was dressed? Because of his mother's arthritis, she hadn't been able to sew a pair of broadfall pants for him or his brothers. For some years now, they'd worn nothing but store-bought jeans. They could have had one of the other women in the community sew them, but they were too afraid to ask for fear of hurting their mother's pride.

Except for his black hat and his accent, she might not think he was Amish at all. The unshaven scruff on his jaw didn't help, but he hadn't thought to run a razor over his face before he left the house. Truthfully, he and his brothers hadn't been much for shaving this winter. Not only had it kept their faces warm, but they'd gotten a little lazy with their appearance, and so far, it seemed to help them sell more trees.

However, It hadn't helped him any when Hannah's father had refused his request to court her properly. He'd claimed Ben and his brothers were unruly and rebellious toward the rules of the *Ordnung*. But since they hadn't yet taken the baptism, the Bishop hadn't raised any questions with them about it. Would he get into the same trouble with the young woman's father if he asked to take her for a buggy ride?

Why am I worried about such narrish things so soon? I haven't even met her officially yet!

Stopping his buggy on the street in front of the bakery, he breathed in the warm scent of cookies and hot cocoa. His stomach growled just thinking about the sweet treats that would warm him after the frigid drive over here.

Tying up his horse, he dropped a few coins into the meter on the street and went to the back of his buggy for the evergreen wreath he'd made to give to the woman as a welcome gift. He glanced up at the door, thinking it looked plain and could use a bit of Christmas cheer.

They probably haven't had time to decorate for the holidays yet, but this wreath should make it more festive.

Pulling in a deep breath, he straightened the red velvet bow on the wreath and headed toward the scent of cinnamon and sugar that made his mouth water, wondering if the young woman he sought out would be just as welcoming as the tempting aroma coming from her shop.

CHAPTER TWO

Ben straightened the red velvet ribbon once more to make sure it was presentable. The woman could hardly turn away a man who was bearing a gift, could she?

He'd learned the skill of making the wreaths from his mother, who used to make them when they were younger. Since their father's death, the boys had taken over the business entirely, and their mother's arthritis had not allowed her to make any more wreaths. She'd been proud that she was able to pass her talent on to her son, but Ben always thought his mother's handiwork with the evergreens and the ribbon was just a little bit better than his.

Two generations before them had used the tree farm to feed their families, but Ben and his brothers had made it what it was today—by expanding their sales with the tree lot so they could appeal to the *Englishers* who were no longer interested in cutting down their own trees. Family ventures to their tree farm to cut down their Christmas tree had become a thing of the past. *Englishers* seemed to want everything done for them, and Ben and his brothers had needed to accommodate them to compete for sales.

Truthfully, their family had the best trees around for miles. Some would even cross the state line to get one of their trees. Not only were they reasonably priced, but they went that extra mile and often tied them down on the tops of the *Englisher's* cars. And they always served hot chocolate and homemade cookies. For the next few weeks, Ben thought they should get the cookies from the bakery since his mother was unable to stand at the stove for too long, or her sprained ankle would swell.

Maybe for the next week or so, I could work out some sort of barter with the new owners of the bakery.

As he neared the door, he knew just what he could help them with; the whole place was devoid of Christmas decorations and greenery. Paying for cookies every day would get to be pretty expensive and would cut into their profits, but if he traded a tree and other greenery, perhaps they could make it work.

Ben walked into the bakery with a smile on his face and a bounce to his step, feeling eager to strike a deal with the beautiful young woman he could see behind the counter in the kitchen.

The jingling of the bells on the door brought her eyes up from her work, and she greeted him with a smile that nearly melted all the snow from him.

He let his gaze wander from the empty dining room to the back, where she seemed to be the only one in the bakery.

"Are you open yet?" he asked.

She wiped her hands on her apron and walked around from the kitchen to meet him at the counter. "*Jah,* we are open, but no customers yet. You look like you could use something hot to warm you up."

Ben nodded and smiled. "*Danki,* I would like a cup of hot chocolate."

Ben looked around again at the empty dining room while she made his hot cocoa. He knew it was still early in the morning, but he could remember seeing the line out the door at this place some days.

"I suppose it takes a while for customers to know you are open for business," she said, handing him the cup. Her porcelain cheeks turned pink when their fingers touched. She cast her eyes down, but he delighted in her shyness with him. "The previous owner promised us he had an overabundance of regular customers, but I suppose it might take them a while to get used to buying from the Amish."

"The *Englishers* will buy from you— just like they buy our Christmas trees, but you have to meet them half-way."

Holly folded her arms over her middle and looked at him blankly. "Meet them half-way?"

Ben held up the wreath in his free hand and smiled. "The previous owners always bought a lot of greenery from our tree farm, and they put the biggest tree right over there in the corner," he said, pointing with his finger. "The place didn't just smell *gut,* but it looked festive—Christmassy."

"I would love to do all of that traditional decorating, but this is *mei vadder's* first business, and he's pretty strict about expenses."

Ben smiled and pulled off his other glove and extended his hand to the beautiful young woman. She took it slowly, and the warmth sent tingles up to his elbow. He felt his cheeks warm, and he almost forgot his own name and why he was there.

He cleared his throat and let her hand slip from his so he could think more clearly. "I'm Benjamin Bontrager. As I mentioned, *mei familye* owns a tree farm, and *mei mudder* is currently having to stay off a sprained ankle. Since I need some cookies to give to our customers for about a week or so while she's resting. I thought we might be able to help each other out. I'd be willing to trade a tree and some greenery to decorate your bakery for the cookies because truthfully, our budget is a little tight too."

He held up the wreath again to show her. "I could make a few smaller wreaths to put them up across the front of the counter, and we could put a big tree in that corner just like the previous owners did. I'd even be willing to tell my customers where we got the cookies and give them a handout that tells about your bakery. If you'd be willing to do the same for us about the tree, we can cross-promote each other's businesses."

Her smile brightened, and Ben felt the cold melt right off him.

"I'm Holly Yoder; it's nice to meet you, and that sounds like a *gut* idea!"

"Holly?" he asked without meaning to.

Should I tell her I'd already nicknamed her Holly because of the color of her eyes?

"*Mei mudder* named me Holly because of the color of my eyes," she said with a giggle. "That and I was born on Christmas Eve."

Ben chuckled inwardly at her statement.

Lord, if that's a sign from you that I was meant to come here this morning to meet her, I'm glad I followed my instincts.

"I have to agree with your *mudder's* choice for naming you," Ben said, smiling. "It's a beautiful name."

He wanted to add that it was a beautiful name for a beautiful woman, but he didn't want to appear forward and prideful.

"*Danki,*" she said. "I'm sure if we make a deal—about the cookies and the tree, *mei vadder* won't mind."

"We open the tree lot to the public every night at five o'clock," he said. "It's at the other end of the block. Can you have the cookies ready by then each day?"

"*Jah,* how many will you need?"

"*Mei mudder* usually bakes about three dozen each day. Is that too much?"

"*Nee,*" she said with a giggle. "I could deliver them if you'd like me to."

"You don't have to do that," he said. "I would be happy to come to pick them up on my way into town with the trees. We cut and net them during the day and then bring a load in the evenings. We have a flatbed trailer we use to haul them."

"That sounds like a lot of work," she said.

"It is, but it keeps us warm while we're out there."

"I'd love to see the tree farm," she said, her lashes dropping.

Ben could see a hint of pink in her cheeks, and it made him smile internally, thinking she might be interested in him the way he was attracted to her.

"You and your *vadder* are welcome to take supper with us tonight so we can discuss the arrangement with our parents," he said.

"What about your *mudder's* ankle?" Holly asked. "Should I bring some things to share for the meal, so she won't have to work so hard?"

"That's mostly why I'm here," Ben said with a chuckle. "To purchase a few pies and loaves of bread. She can manage supper with a little bit of help from me, but the doctor advised her to stay off her ankle for at least a week. I thought that if I could get some baked goods for her, it would make things easier."

"I won't have you paying for those things," Holly said with a smile. "If we will be your guests, I'll bring the sweets and bread as my contribution."

Ben smiled. "*Danki;* see you and your *vadder* at six o'clock."

She nodded and returned his smile. "That's perfect since we close at five."

"Do you want me to hang this on your front door?" Ben asked.

Holly nodded and giggled. "I would like that very much. I think it might liven the place up a bit. *Mei mudder* loved Christmas, but *dat* moved us away so we wouldn't have to spend another Christmas without her in our *haus* back in Grabill."

"Is that why you moved to our community?" Ben asked.

She handed him some twine, and he tied a piece to the back of the wreath.

"*Jah, mei vadder* couldn't work the farm anymore and wanted a business and a place in town to live. We have a nice loft upstairs, and if we can get some of those regular customers in, we can make a fine living here. We couldn't scratch a living out of that farm the past few years. Last year, a hailstorm wiped out our crops, and I believe that was what made up *mei dat's* mind that farming was no longer for him. So, here we are."

Ben smiled and picked up the wreath and headed for the door. "I'm glad you chose our community."

She smiled shyly and cast her eyes down.

"I'll get this hung, and then I'll be on my way, he said. "*Mei brudders* will be missing me."

"*Danki,* for the invitation to supper, but I'm afraid I don't know where you live."

Ben felt his face turn warm. "I forgot you're new here!" he said, trying to cover up his embarrassment. "If you follow Main Street out of town going west, you'll run into our farm about four miles down the road. The *haus* is to the left at the end of the road. You can't miss all the pine trees behind us. They go back quite a ways."

She smiled. "I can't wait to see it."

"I'll let *mei mudder* know to expect a few extras tonight for supper, but she always makes enough food to feed us more than twice," he said with a chuckle.

Holly moved from around the counter to be nearer to him at the door. Folding her arms around her middle, she shivered from the cold air he was letting inside the bakery.

He hung the wreath and looked up at her and waited for approval.

"It looks like Christmas!" she said. "How many siblings do you have?"

"I have three *brudders,*" he answered. "Luke is my twin—older than I am by a few minutes, and he's never let me forget it. Simon is the second born, and Jonas, our youngest *brudder,* is out among the *English* on his *rumspringa.* We're hoping he'll come home for Christmas—for *mei mudder's* sake. She misses him."

Ben closed the door and took another sip of hot cocoa from his to-go cup. "What about you? Do you have any sisters or brothers to help you in the bakery?"

She shook her head. "*Nee,* it's only me and *mei dat.* After *mei mudder* had me, the doctor told her she couldn't have anymore *kinner.*"

"*Ach,* I'm sorry about that," he said.

"I have a cousin my age who will be here in a few days to help me with the baking, but if we don't get more customers in here, she might not be needed."

Ben thought about his brothers having another fresh face in the community and figured it might not be such a bad idea if they decided to take an interest in Holly when they had supper together. He'd have to remind them her cousin was on her way.

"I'll help you get those customers in here," he said with cheer in his tone. "The two of you will have more than enough work to keep you busy."

"I pray you're right about that," she said with a smile.

He hated to leave, but Luke would wonder what was taking him so long.

"But *Dat,* I already accepted the invitation," Holly argued. "If we didn't show up for supper at the Bontrager's *haus,* it wouldn't be polite!"

"Silas is expecting to take you for a buggy ride this evening," her father said sternly.

"Fiddlesticks!" Holly said under her breath. "Silas might have to wait. The Bontrager family has made us a generous offer to help us sell more at the bakery and turning the regular customers back toward us."

"This attitude of your would not have something to do with the fact the Widow Bontrager has four young *menner* of marrying age, would it?" her father asked with a stern tone.

Holly bit her bottom lip. "*Nee;* Ben made a kind offer, and that's all."

He paused, seemingly staring right through her. "Just remember that you're betrothed."

I wish I could forget it!

"I think you should make it clear to Ben that you're not interested right from the start—so he won't get any ideas about the two of you," her father said.

"What if I am interested?" Holly asked.

"You'll have to put those feelings away," he said. "You've been promised to Silas."

"*You* promised me to Silas," she corrected him. "I didn't promise him anything."

"Don't sass me!" her father scolded her.

Holly bit back tears. "Don't you care if I'm happy or not?"

Hiram Yoder wiped his hands on a towel and looked at her thoughtfully. "Of course, I do. I only want what's best for you."

"Then why don't you let me choose my own husband?" she asked. "Making me marry Silas is not what's best for me; it's what's best for you."

"I did that for you," he said sternly. "I didn't want you growing old on that farm and using up all of your youth to care for me and work so hard that you miss your chance to marry and have *kinner.*"

The thought of having children with Silas brought bile up her throat. "I want to fall in love like you and *mamm.*"

"Our marriage was arranged," he reminded her. "You can learn to love Silas; love takes time."

"Or sometimes it just happens when you don't expect it to," she said with a sing-song voice.

"You are treading on dangerous waters if you think you have the freedom to give your heart to Ben Bontrager," he barked. "Perhaps we should skip this supper invitation so you can keep a safe distance from this young *mann.*"

"Nee, Dat," she cried. "It would be rude if we didn't show up."

"I don't want to make any bad relationships in our new community," her father grumbled. "But don't do accept any more invitations without checking with me first."

Holly smiled and bounced on her heels. "I won't."

"Stop looking so happy about seeing this young *mann,* or I'll change my mind."

Holly bit her lip to suppress her giddiness about seeing Ben; if she couldn't keep her emotions in check, she'd ruin what could be the first of many encounters with Ben.

Hiram let out a sigh. "Let's get this kitchen cleaned up so we can be on our way. They will be expecting us, and we don't want to be impolite by arriving late."

Holly reached her flour-covered hands around her father's neck and hugged him.

"*Danki, Dat.*"

"For what?" he asked.

"For not fighting me on this," she said.

"I only want to make sure you aren't stalling to take that first buggy ride with Silas."

Holly resisted the urge to curl her lip at the mention of her cousin. Instead, she pasted on a smile and let her father's comment drop. There was no use arguing with the man, but that didn't mean she wouldn't do everything in her power to put off Silas for as long as she could get away with it.

CHAPTER THREE

Ben helped his mother to get supper on the table and set extra places for their guests.

"She must be very beautiful for you to be going through so much trouble," his mother said with a knowing smile.

Ben couldn't hide his excitement from his mother; she knew him too well.

"My son is ready to settle down and start a *familye* of his own, *jah?*" she asked.

His smile widened. "I am."

"Then I will welcome Holly and do everything I can to help," she said. "I have been waiting a lot of years for a *dochder.*"

He kissed his mother's cheek. "I know you have, *Mamm.*"

The clip-clop of horse's hooves in the driveway alerted them that their guests had arrived. He and his brothers had cleared the driveway of fresh snow so that Holly and her father would have an easy path up their steep driveway.

"I'll go out and unhitch their horse," Ben said. "Will you be alright inside with our company until I get back?"

It suddenly struck him that he had invited a widower to take supper with them, but he prayed his mother would not see it as a setup because he hadn't meant it that way.

"I'll be fine," she said, wiping her hands on her apron. He caught her smoothing her hair behind her *kapp* and wondered if his mother might suspect the invitation could have been just as much for her benefit as it was for Ben.

"I'll hurry!" he said, shouldering into his coat. His main concern was to make a good impression on the man he hoped would be his future father-in-law.

Luckily, he made it out the door before the man parked his buggy, which allowed him the chance to offer a hand to assist him down.

"It's a little slippery out here," he said to the man as he helped him out of his buggy. "I'm Ben; we're pleased you'll be having supper with us."

The man nodded, and then Ben offered his hand to Holly, who greeted him with a nervous smile. It was a smile that conveyed to him that her father might not be on board with the invitation for some reason. Did he think they were trying to set him up with his widowed mother? He prayed not, but he wasn't going to bring it up just in case he was wrong.

Who knows? Maybe Holly was just nervous, and he was reading too much into her expression. He'd not had any experience around women unless you could count his time spent with cousins, but he didn't think that amounted for much. He had no romantic feelings for them—not like he had for Holly.

He was indeed pleased to see her, even if her father had accompanied her. He hoped they could steal away for a moment alone after supper so he could invite her to take a sleigh ride with him in the moonlight.

First, he would get through supper, and hopefully, his mother could keep her father occupied with coffee and pie afterward to give Ben some time with Holly.

At least that was his plan.

Holly felt a little shaky when her father flashed her a look after she took Ben's hand and allowed him to help her down from the buggy. Normally, she would let herself down, but she had eagerly taken Ben's hand, the warmth of it permeating her knitted mittens. She'd have to remember that her father would watch her every move during this visit, but she'd prayed she'd get a moment alone with Ben this evening. She'd taken a liking to him almost instantly, and the few minutes she'd spent with him at the bakery earlier had left her wanting more.

She followed Ben toward the house, smiling when he looked back at her before opening the back door for her father. It was warm in the kitchen, and the aroma of roast beef and red potatoes welcomed her.

"Let me take your coat, Mr. Yoder," Ben said.

He nodded and shrugged out of his waistcoat, and Ben looked to Holly with an outstretched hand waiting for her long, wool coat.

She stuffed her mittens in the pockets and then untied her winter bonnet, leaving her hair a little messy under her white prayer *kapp.* She tucked the stray reddish tendrils behind her ear while Ben watched, her father's coat still folded over his arm. He finally managed to break his gaze away long enough to hang up the coats on the pegs against the back wall by the door.

After the introductions, she noticed her father and Ben's mother seemed a little distracted by each other. "Please—sit," his mother stammered. "Let me get you a cup of *kaffi* to warm you up." Then she turned her attention toward Holly and smiled warmly. "Would you like one, dear?"

Holly smiled and nodded. "*Danki, jah,* but I'd like to help serve the meal," she offered. "Tell me what I can do to help."

Frau Bontrager patted her arm and flashed her son a look. "I like her already!"

What did she mean by that?

Ben sat with Holly's father at the kitchen table, and the two began to discuss the offer he'd made at the bakery. She planned to stay out of it and give them time to talk and get to know one another, hoping it might change her father's mind about letting her choose her own future husband. She had no idea if Ben was interested in her the way she was in him, but she suspected he might be from the way he smiled at her.

Frau Bontrager welcomed Holly into her kitchen, and it was a refreshing change for her after being without a mother for more than a year. She'd spent the past two weeks baking with her father, teaching him how to knead bread and ice cookies, she'd almost forgotten what it was like to work with a woman who knew her way around the kitchen.

Not to mention how nice it was to have a mother figure. The woman was kind and welcoming the way her own mother was. Her aunt Miriam, Silas' mother, was not a kind woman, and Holly knew she would have a miserable time if the woman became her mother-in-law, if her father forced her to marry Silas.

Holly shook off the stressful thoughts; she was here to have a nice evening with the handsome man who'd surprised her at the bakery earlier. There was no sense in borrowing trouble now when she could be enjoying herself in the widow's company, and hopefully Ben's too.

Then a thought occurred to her. If she could get her father to spend more time with

Ben's mother, perhaps it would open the door for her to spend more time with Ben. Her father had been awfully lonely this past year, and *Frau* Bontrager would make a perfect wife for her father. Would it be wrong for her to encourage him to court the widow?

With Ben at her back, she felt a little nervous, but he was so engrossed in his conversation with her father that she was glad for the time with his mother.

"I understand you bought the bakery in town, *jah?*" his mother asked.

Holly poured out the Mason jar of chow-chow into a serving bowl and looked up to answer. "*Jah,* we sold our farm and used the proceeds to purchase the bakery. We live in the loft above the bakery."

"Do you like it so far?"

Holly giggled. "It's almost more work than plowing, planting, and harvesting.

Working with hot ovens all day is almost like working in the hot sun all day."

The older woman smiled. "I can imagine so. If I had to spend the entire day baking, I'd be tired."

"The only real difference between the two is that we don't have to rely on nature to provide us with crops," Holly said. "But we haven't yet gotten many customers."

"Is that what they're talking about?" the woman asked, motioning to her son and Holly's father.

The two men had their heads together at the table and were deep in conversation.

Holly nodded and smiled. "Your son has some *gut* ideas about helping us get the regular customers back inside the bakery. They haven't been in much since we took over the place."

Mrs. Bontrager put a comforting hand on Holly's arm. "Don't worry; if there is a way to make your business bring in more profit for you, my Ben can do that. He's the one who put our tree farm in business."

Holly giggled. "He wants to bring some of that to our bakery."

"Let him decorate your place and make it look like Christmas; you won't be sorry, and it will draw in the customers," she said.

Holly giggled. "That's exactly what he told me."

"Then you should listen to him; he's a wise young *mann.*"

"*Ach,* if he can convince *mei vadder,* that will be a miracle," Holly said.

"Then it's a miracle we'll be praying for," his mother said with a smile.

Holly really liked her; not only was she understanding, but she was sweeter than honey, just like her own mother was.

Mrs. Bontrager lifted the roast from the oven and set it on the stovetop while Holly stirred gravy for the potatoes and carrots.

"*Danki* for bringing the buttermilk biscuits and pie for supper," his mother said.

"It's the least I could contribute," Holly said. "That roast is making my mouth water."

"If my youngest son were here tonight, we'd all be lucky if we got one little piece of that roast," she said with a sad smile. "He could eat this entire roast on his own."

"Ben told me he was away on *rumspringa*. Do you miss him?" Holly asked.

"*Jah,* but I'm praying he will come home for Christmas," she answered soulfully.

"Why don't you get off your feet for a few minutes and I'll serve supper," Holly offered.

Mrs. Bontrager waved a hand at her. "I'm fine! My son and the doctor make more fuss over my sprained ankle than need be."

"I'd feel better if you'd let me help," Holly practically insisted.

The woman put a hand under Holly's chin and smiled. "I can see why my Ben likes you; you're a kind young woman."

Holly hadn't expected to hear that. She bit her bottom lip to keep from gasping until the woman let go of her face. She flashed her one more smile and then sat with the men, leaving Holly at the counter, scrambling to remember what she was doing. If his own mother knew he liked her, then maybe, just maybe, she had a chance to win his heart.

CHAPTER FOUR

Ben was pleased with how well their supper together was turning out. Neither of his brothers had embarrassed him so far, and his mother seemed to get along better with Holly's father than he'd hoped for. But there was more to it than that; his mother liked Holly and approved of her, and that meant a lot to him.

He waited for a lull in the conversation and then addressed Holly. "Would you like to come back tomorrow morning and pick out the tree for the bakery?"

She dropped her fork and covered her full mouth, her eyes darting nervously between her father and Ben, but she nodded before her father had a chance to object; Ben could see reprimand in his eyes, and he wasn't going to give the man a chance to put a damper on his plans.

"What about the batch of bread we need to bake in the morning?" he asked his daughter with a firm tone.

She finished chewing and smiled nervously. "You can do that, *Dat;* I already made the dough and rolled it up and put it in the walk-in. All you have to do is bring the rack of pans out to let the dough rise and then put them in the oven an hour later."

She'd made it easy for her father to agree and accept, but he'd hesitated just long enough to make Ben wonder if he was going to forbid Holly to make the trip back here to pick out the tree.

"I can stay until all the bread is in the oven and then come out here after I've got everything all set up for you," she offered.

"Once you get into a routine with baking bread, it's so easy it's almost fun!" Ben's mother chimed in. "I'd be more than happy to walk you through it; I can't be on my feet, but I can give you some direction."

The man flashed a sideways glance at *Frau* Bontrager and then smiled. "*Nee,* that won't be necessary; I think I can handle it alone. After all, I'm the one who decided to open the bakery. It's probably best if I learn to be on my own once in a while since I'll have to work it alone when Holly gets married."

Holly's cheeks turned red hot, and she lowered her gaze. Ben darted his gaze between Holly and her father. Why did he have to go there? Did this man intend to shame his daughter in front of strangers and remind her that she was still unmarried at her age? Though most of the young women in their community were married by age eighteen, she still had plenty of time—and one willing bachelor right in front of her.

The look she flashed her father practically begged him to keep his mouth shut about the subject, but there seemed to be more to it than that. Ben was certain that Holly didn't want her personal issues being talked about in front of him. The two appeared to be at odds over the subject of marriage, but did he mention her single status in front of Ben as a hint he was he trying to match her up with him right now? If he was, no wonder the poor girl was embarrassed. The man didn't need to sell Holly to Ben; he was already interested in her.

Ben sent Holly a compassionate smile that made his heart thump harder against his ribs. But he couldn't help but notice the sadness in Holly's eyes at her father's statement. Was it possible she was already betrothed to someone? *Ach*, but how could she be? They'd only just moved to the community a couple of weeks ago. He hadn't heard anything amongst his peers that would have him believe she had someone here waiting to marry her. As far he knew, they had relatives here, but no one else seemed to know them. Unless she had someone back home in Grabill, and he would be joining them soon.

Ben shook off the feeling as a possible misunderstanding of Holly's expression but wished he could convey his interest in her for courting. If he could not talk to her tonight, her father had reluctantly given his permission for her to come back to the farm tomorrow. Perhaps then would be a better time for Ben to invite her to take a buggy ride with him.

It was apparent that Mr. Yoder's interest in his mother could work to his advantage in having some time alone with Holly. Even his mother seemed to be lost in Mr. Yoder's company, and he was pleased to see her smiling again, especially with Christmas right around the corner. He knew it was one of the many times throughout the past year that made her miss his father the most. They hadn't celebrated his birthday, and there hadn't been any mention of their anniversary this year.

Ben had prayed for his mother to be happy again, even if that meant she would remarry. He and his brothers were grown and too old to worry about having a stepfather. If she married, she would be happy and taken care of, and then maybe he and his brothers would not have to feel guilty about wanting to get married themselves.

It didn't take long for his brothers to excuse themselves from the table, and though Ben knew he should get out to the barn to help them with chores, he felt compelled to stay and keep Holly company.

"I noticed when we drove up that you have goats in a pen," Holly said to him. "Would it be alright if I went out to see them?"

Ben leapt from his chair. "*Jah,* I'd be happy to show them to you."

She hesitated once more and waited for her father to give her a nod. He did, but it was reserved—scolding almost, as if he'd given permission only because she'd put him on the spot. Ben wasn't too concerned about what his reasons were; he was happy for the chance to spend some time alone with the beautiful woman who made his heart beat at an exhilarating pace.

At the back door, Ben helped her into her coat and noticed it brought pink to her cheeks. He liked that she was shy; he was normally shy too, but he felt comfortable with her—as if he'd known her most of his life. He prayed she would come to be as comfortable with him. He was certain her nervousness had more to do with her father being there with her. Earlier, when he'd seen her alone at the bakery, she seemed a lot more relaxed and open. The true test of their compatibility would be in time spent alone—away from her father's stern looks. He wasn't sure what that was about, but maybe he was leery of them because they were so new to the community.

"How many acres do you have?" Holly asked once they were out into the cold night.

"A little over seven hundred," he answered. "Before *mei vadder* passed away, he sectioned out some of the land for me and *mei brudders* to build our own homes. He gave us each fifteen acres so that we can have plenty of room for chickens and a large kitchen garden without being on top of each other."

"Your farmland does seem to go on for miles," she said.

Ben chuckled. "It's not that large, but it does maintain itself for the most part," Ben answered. "Every spring, we replant saplings to replace what we cut down the previous winter. By the time we get around to those trees, they'll be ten years grown. Our *dat* taught us how to rotate the trees and to always replace what you cut down."

"I guess you need that many acres to make the farm work for you," she said.

He nodded. "That way, we're always growing. We even sell the wood chips in the spring from leftover branches and grinding the stumps."

"Sounds like your *vadder* left you a *gut* legacy," she said.

"Isn't your *dat* doing the same for you with the bakery?"

She bit her bottom lip and hesitated. "I thought so, but when he sold our farm and bought the bakery, I think it was more for himself. But I know if he had his way, I'd never have to get married, and I'd be able to work by his side for the rest of his life."

"*Have* to get married?" Ben asked. He wasn't going to ask, but he had to know.

Her cheeks turned bright red, and her eyes cast down. "You know what I mean."

Ben wasn't sure what she meant by her comment, but he let it drop since it seemed to cause her agitation, and he wanted her visit to be a pleasant one. He didn't have any sisters, but he had cousins, and he'd never heard any of them refer to marriage as *having* to get married. He let out a breath, watching it crystalize in the icy air in front of him, determined to let it go for now. If it was something to be worried about, he'd deal with it when and if it presented itself as a problem.

They reached the goat pen beside the barn, and she giggled as she bent to extend a hand to a young doe that neared the fence to greet them with happy bleats. The sun was nearly down, but it was still light enough that the little goats wagged their tails happily as they approached.

She reached between the fence wire to pet the eager little doe. "*Ach,* I miss my goats back home, and I could sure use them now for milk and to make cheese for the bakery."

"She's one of mine," Ben said, pointing to the young doe. "I'd be happy to trade you some milk from her on a regular basis. I'm sure we could come to some sort of agreement in exchange for bread and pie, and such."

"You won't need those things for long," she said. "Your *mamm* will be on her feet full time again soon. Besides, I have a feeling she might be getting them from *mei dat* if the way they got along at supper was any indication of a friendship between them."

"I think they like each other," Ben said. "Is that alright with you?"

She nodded without looking at him. "If it keeps him busy and happy, I'm all for it."

Busy? Didn't her father have enough to do with his new business? Or was it more keeping out of Holly's business that she was concerned about?

"When she drops in the spring, she'll give a lot of milk, but I have an older one I can gift to you; she'll give milk for a long time because her *kinner* are over a year old."

Her eyes locked onto his with a shocked expression. Ben panicked; was that the wrong thing to say?

"Why would you give her to me?" she asked quietly, her eyes fixed on the young doe.

He shrugged, not wanting to tell her the real reason behind his gift. "You seem to need a *gut* milking goat—for the bakery."

"I don't have anywhere to keep her," she said.

"I can keep her here for you, and you can come over and get milk from her when you need it," Ben offered.

She smiled shyly, as if she suddenly realized he was looking for a reason to keep her coming back to visit him. She understood his intentions, but he was not ready to admit he'd prefer to offer the goat as an engagement gift. It was probably too soon for that, but the more time he spent with her would give him that answer.

Holly felt her heart speed up when Ben mentioned giving her the goat. Why did she have to meet him *after* her father had promised her to Silas? Why did he have to be so kind and gentle—and so interested in her? She wanted to explore where her attraction to Ben could take them, but unless she was able to talk her father into letting her out of the promise he'd made for her hand, she was wasting her time with Ben. It would only make her heart grow fond of him and want him more when it could never be.

Why couldn't I have met Ben before now, Lord?

She swallowed down a sadness knowing she would never know what true love felt like. Having to marry a man she didn't love was not what she wanted for her future. The only way she could choose her own husband now would be if she went against her father's wishes, and then Silas would surely have her shunned for rejecting him. Then she would never be able to court Ben. He was part of the community and everything she'd known her whole life. She didn't have the stomach for trying to make her way in the *English* world, and she highly doubted Ben would follow her there; he had a family here and land that had been handed down from his deceased father.

Unless…unless his mudder marries mei dat. Maybe then he'll feel an obligation to Ben instead of Silas.

But there would still be a matter of the money her father borrowed from his cousin. How would she ever make enough money to pay him back? Would paying him back get her out of marrying Silas?

It might be the only way I can seek out my feelings for Ben.

"Where are you?" Ben asked, putting a hand on her arm.

Holly jumped.

"You were a million miles away!" he said.

She felt her cheeks turn warm. She didn't dare tell him that her mind had wandered to taking a buggy ride with him.

"I was just thinking of where I could keep the goat," she said.

"I like the idea of keeping her here," he said with a smile. "That way, I get to see you often."

She straightened up from her haunches where she'd been petting the goat. "I don't think *mei dat* will allow me to come here and milk a goat."

"Why not?" Ben asked. "You're an adult; does he keep that tight of a hold on you still?"

Nee, but the arrangement he made could get me shunned if I don't follow through with it!

Holly bit her bottom lip and looked away from him. "It's just won't work out, Ben," she said, her voice breaking. "I'm sorry; I better go."

Ben stood there with his mouth hanging open as she walked back toward the house. She knew if she stayed there any longer, her heart would break from wanting a man she could never have.

CHAPTER FIVE

Ben got up a little earlier than usual, hoping to finish his chores so he'd have enough time to run an errand before Holly showed up. Though they'd had a bit of a falling out, before she and her father went home, she'd promised to see him at ten o'clock this morning. Time would tell if she changed her mind or not, as women were often known to do. She had run hot and cold with him last night, and he worried he might have pushed things a little too far with his flirting and spooked her.

It was a frigid morning, but the snow was light, making traveling easier for Holly. If it had been coming down thick, he had made up his mind to go fetch her and drive her back to his farm. But the day looked promising for only light snow well into the afternoon. By the end of the day, the accumulation could amount to enough that he and his brothers might have to shovel the driveway again, but he prayed not. He had too much to do today to be bothered with the chore.

"Where are you off to so early?" Luke asked him.

Ben held his hands up to his mouth and blew warm air over the tips of his cold fingers before putting on his gloves. He had only a short ride down the road, but it was only about twelve degrees today.

"I have an errand to run," he said.

"Does this errand have anything to do with Holly Yoder?"

Ben frowned at his twin. Luke was always getting in Ben's business, and he didn't want Luke sticking his nose in this, of all things.

"What if it does?"

Luke clucked his tongue. "I heard she's promised to Silas Yoder."

Ben felt his heart slam against his ribs. "Where did you hear that?"

"From some of the guys in the youth group," Luke warned.

"That can't be true; they're cousins, ain't it so?" Ben shot back.

"They're third cousins, and that's allowed."

Ben pursed his lips. "Until I hear it from Holly herself, I'm going to assume she's available for courting."

"That might be what her father meant last night at supper when he talked about *when* she gets married."

Ben remembered Holly's comment about *having* to get married. Was it possible her father was forcing her into a marriage of convenience? But for whose convenience?

Did Ben have the right to rescue her from such a fate? Or the guts?

He shrugged it off. There was no use worrying about a rumor.

"I'll be back before she gets here," Ben said. "Don't question her about what you heard. I don't want her thinking this community is full of nothing but gossips!"

Luke chuckled. "Do you think if you don't know the truth that will make it go away, and you can still court her?"

"If she wants me to court her, I will," Ben said, slapping at the reins.

His horse took off slowly down the icy driveway toward the home of the community seamstress. He planned to surprise Holly by wearing broadfall pants and suspenders. He hoped that looking a little less *English* might make a difference in his quest for Holly. At least it might help to change her father's mind about him as a suitable match for his daughter.

By the time Ben reached home, he had only a few minutes to change his clothes before Holly arrived. It was a good thing he'd gotten up early, or he might have missed her visit with his last-minute errand. If *Frau*

Miller hadn't needed to hem the bottom of the pants, he would have been home sooner, but at least he'd made it in time.

After he changed, he went through the kitchen where his mother stopped him.

"I see you've paid a visit to *Frau* Miller."

Ben nodded. "*Jah,* I thought it might be time to retire my blue jeans," he said.

"I feel I should warn you that Holly is betrothed." his mother said.

Ben felt his blood run cold. "How do you know that?"

"Mr. Yoder told me last night while the two of you were outside looking at the goats," she answered.

The man must have suspected he was interested in his daughter and felt the need to end it before anything got started between them, but he was too late. Ben was all-in with his heart. He collapsed into the nearest chair. "So, it's true then."

His mother sat across from him and patted his hand and smiled soberly. "Her father told me that he made a promise for her hand, and she is rebelling against the match."

Ben's face lit up with a smile. "She is?"

"I don't think you should encourage her to rebel against her *vadder*," his mother warned. "There is a lot at stake; his cousin Henry put up the money for them to purchase the bakery, and in exchange, he promised Holly to marry Silas, Henry's son."

"So, he is her cousin, then?" he asked.

His mother nodded. "Her third cousin."

"No wonder she made that comment about *having* to get married," Ben said. "I *know* she doesn't want to marry her cousin."

"What makes you think that?"

"For one thing," he said, smiling with confidence. "I think she likes me!"

Holly steered her buggy into the Bontrager's driveway. She was eager to see Ben; she liked him despite the fact he was *forbidden* under the circumstances. If only she hadn't pushed her father to sell their farm and relocate to this community. Then she wouldn't be facing a forced marriage to Cousin Silas.

However, she wouldn't have met Ben either. Surely, God would not have brought her here just so she could get her heart broken.

Ben exited the house and greeted her with a weak smile and a wave, causing her heart to speed up. Did he know her secret? Of course, it wouldn't be a secret for much longer if her father had his way. By this time next week, she suspected the entire community would know she was being forced into a marriage with her third cousin.

Her stomach knotted up. Maybe she should have gone light on the breakfast before coming here. If Ben had this kind of effect on her every time she saw him, she was going to stay knotted up the whole morning.

She pulled in a deep breath just before Ben approached her buggy and breathed out a prayer asking God for wisdom to know what to do about her feelings for Ben. She had been instantly attracted to his looks and charm yesterday, and she'd barely gotten any sleep last night thinking about his kindness and devotion to his family. A family he would never leave behind to be with her if she got herself shunned for rejecting Silas.

With his coat still open, she noticed his suspenders and the broadfall pants right away. But there was something else different about him; he'd shaven his face, though he'd left what looked like a little stubble. She liked the scruffy look on him, but his beard had been a little too thick yesterday for her liking. He had a strong square jaw, and his kind brown eyes smiled up at her from where she sat in her buggy. Were his changes for her sake?

"I'm so glad you made it this morning," he said, widening his smile. "It's a cold morning, ain't it so?"

He was glad to see her; that was a good sign, wasn't it?

Ben reached for her hand and assisted her down to the snowy ground, her feet slipping on the ice. She squealed, but he caught her in his strong arms and paused to hold her briefly.

Her breath hitched, but she stifled it. Snowflakes whirled around them and lighted on her lashes, but it wasn't the weight of them that caused her lashes to flutter; it was his strong, warm embrace that held her heart captive.

"I'm sorry," he said, clearing his throat. "I should have thrown down a little rock salt to keep this path clear of ice. Let me take your hand, and we'll walk to the edge of the path where there isn't any ice."

She nodded, not wanting him to let go, but he did. But then he took her arm and tucked it in the crook of his elbow, placing his free hand over hers. The path was slippery, but she'd braved icy paths before on her own; this way was much nicer. She would milk his gentlemanly nature for as long as she could.

"Have you lived here all your life?" she thought to ask, trying to drown out the sound of crunching snow beneath their feet.

"*Nee,* we came from Ohio when Luke and I were five years old," he said, his breath rolling out in front of him in the frigid air with an icy cloud. "*Mei vadder* answered an advertisement for the sale of the farm. It had been handed down for four generations, but the previous owner had no more living relatives and needed to sell because he was getting on in years, and the *haus* was in terrible disrepair. We fixed it up and began to use the trees as our crop, and it has worked for us ever since."

"The previous owners never sold the trees?" she asked.

"*Nee,* the man loved the trees and didn't know about rotating crops, and that you could use the same method with this many acres of trees."

"Sounds like your *vadder* was a smart business *mann.*"

"*Jah,* he was," Ben answered. "He taught me everything I know."

"*Mei mudder* and I used to bake every day," she said. "She taught me everything I know. That's why *Dat* bought the bakery, and now I'm teaching him everything I know. It's funny how that can get so turned around."

He chuckled. "It's always a *gut* thing when the student becomes the teacher."

"I suppose," she said. "But I'd rather be in the kitchen with *mamm;* is that so awful?"

"*Nee,* I miss felling trees with *mei dat,"* he said. "Besides, you never outgrow your parents."

She paused for a minute and then added. "I enjoyed being in the kitchen with your *mudder* last night."

Ben smiled and patted her hand. "She enjoyed your company too; she didn't have any *dochders* of her own. She's been waiting for her boys to be of marrying age so she could have *dochders.*"

Holly's breath hitched again at the mention of marriage. Was that a hint he was interested in her?

"Did I say something wrong?"

She cleared her throat. "*Nee,* my foot almost slipped again."

It wasn't a complete lie; she did hit a slippery patch, but it was his comment that affected her so.

He tightened his grip on her arm. "Don't worry; I've got you. But I must warn you that if you go down, I might go down with you!"

"That's comforting!" she said with a giggle.

He chuckled and patted her hand again, sending warm tingles to her heart.

They reached the end of the path, and Ben led her toward a row of trees so tall they towered over Ben's head, and he was at least a foot taller than she was.

"We have some shorter ones on the next row, but since you have twenty-foot ceilings in the bakery, I thought you might want a larger tree."

Holly's eyes widened as she dipped her face toward the trees and breathed in the smell of pine. "That's one of my favorite smells!" she gushed.

Ben chuckled. "Mine too—next to fresh-brewed *kaffi* and the smell of warm snickerdoodles fresh from the oven."

Holly giggled. "I'll have to remember that."

Ben rubbed his hands together greedily and smiled. "Does this mean I can count on some snickerdoodles in my delivery of cookies this evening at the tree lot?"

Holly tore her attention away from the tree to smile at his boyish charm. "Maybe I'll surprise you!"

He chuckled again. "I love surprises!"

She fluttered her lashes. "I'll have to remember that too."

Ben smiled and pointed to the tree beside the one she'd been smelling. "I think this one is perfect; it tapers nicely at the top; don't you think so?"

She nodded and leaned in to breathe in its pine aroma. "I could never get tired of the smell of pine needles."

"I couldn't either," he agreed. "Even if you're not having the best day, it's hard not to smile when you smell them."

"It's just another reminder of how wonderful *Gott* is for giving us such beautiful things on this earth to enjoy," she said with a smile.

Ben smiled. "I was thinking the same thing about you."

Holly felt her heart skip a beat, and she felt warm all over. Was it just her imagination, or was he flirting with her?

Ach, Lord, is there hope after all that I can find love, and I won't have to marry Silas?

Ben revved the chain saw and cut the tree for Holly's Bakery. He was eager to get out of the cold for a little while and spend some time in the warm bakery that was filled with the mouth-watering scent of cinnamon and peppermint. These were two of his favorite holiday smells that helped keep him in a good mood, but the company he kept was certainly doing its part to lift his spirits.

"Do you need a tree stand?" Ben thought to ask.

She nodded slowly. "I think so. I didn't see one in the attic when we moved into the loft above the bakery."

"Well, if you're not sure, then I'm sure you need one. We can pick one up at the tree lot on the way to the bakery."

"I'm sure you're right," she said with a giggle. "We've never put up a tree indoors before."

"Most Amish don't, but we have always had one in the *haus,*" he said. "It isn't against the rules of our *Ordnung,* but most see it as worldly, so they don't put much up except greenery around the fireplace, but most in the community get that and wreaths for their doors from us."

"I'm afraid at the bakery, we have to rely mostly on the *Englishers* for customers since most Amish homes have at least one woman in the *familye* who bakes."

He nodded. "That's why we are going to make the bakery so inviting with the decorations that the *Englishers* will be lined up around the block trying to get some of those cookies and pies you bake so well. That pie you brought for supper last night was the best apple pie I've had in a long time."

She smiled shyly. "*Danki,* it was *mei mudder's* recipe."

"That crust was so tender and tasty I could have eaten the whole thing myself," he said with a chuckle.

"And you would have regretted it today," she said with a snicker.

He patted his trim stomach. "Not me; I'm all muscle!"

She laughed at him. "That would change if you eat too many sweets!"

"I guess I better not marry you then," he said with a wink. "I wouldn't want to lose my muscle to all those sweets you would tempt me with."

Her pink cheeks made him smile; she was beautiful and shy, and he liked that about her.

"What if I promise not to overfeed you too many sweets?" she asked.

Her question was playfully begging, and it made him believe she was flirting with him.

"I might have to hold you to that," he said. "But if I'm portly on our first anniversary, you might have to put me on a diet!"

Holly giggled, her warm breath rolling in front of her face against the icy December air.

"Let's get this tree to the bakery," he said. "We can pick up some lights at the lot and a few lengths of ribbon to make bows for the tree."

"You don't have to go through all that trouble," she said, following him as he dragged the tree through the snow.

He turned around to face her. "You better learn something about me right from the start," he said. "I don't do anything halfway; *mei dat* taught us to do a job until it's finished, and to do it as best you can."

She nodded and smiled, tucking a bit of her reddish hair behind her winter bonnet. "I like a *mann* who is thorough."

He winked at her again and went back to pulling the tree behind him. When he reached the edge of the tree line, he left the tree on the ground and motioned for her to come with him. "No sense in dragging that heavy tree all the way back to the barn; I'll get the buggy, and we can come back for it."

He took her hand without thinking about it but smiled at her. "I wouldn't want you to slip on the icy path. We don't keep it shoveled since it's usually only used by me and my *brudders.*"

"I understand," she said. "I don't mind; it makes me feel protected."

"That's my job as a gentleman," he said.

"I'm glad you're a gentleman," she said. "Another reason to put a check on my list of why I like you."

"You have a list?" he asked with a chuckle.

"All women have a *list!*" she said.

"What kind of list is it?"

"A list of things to check off about a *mann* when you're considering him," she said shyly. "We use it to evaluate every *mann* we meet."

Ben felt his heart fluttering; did she mean she was considering him for *marriage?*

He chuckled inwardly. "So, what's on your list?"

"He must put *Gott* first in his life," she began. "He must be kind, considerate of others, and he must take pride in his work without being prideful. And he must care for his *mudder*; you can tell a lot about a *mann* by the way he treats his *mudder.*"

He smiled. "What about handsome? Don't you want a *mann* you can be attracted to?"

She lowered her gaze and smiled shyly. "Of course, but it's not the first thing on the list. I would rather have a *mann* who is not so handsome on the outside, but who has a beautiful and kind heart."

"Is that your whole list?"

She sighed whimsically. "There are other things on the list, but the most important are kindness, gentleness, and a love for *Gott* and his *familye.*"

"I guess you might as well say yes right now then," he said with a chuckle.

Her breath hitched. "What?"

He puffed out his chest and smiled. "I fit everything on your list—and more. I'd make a *gut* husband." His brown eyes danced with merriment.

He was baiting her, but either she didn't seem to realize it, or she wasn't as interested in him as he'd originally thought.

He helped her into his buggy, and then he climbed up next to her, sitting as close as he dared to sit without being too forward. She shivered a little, and he reached under the seat and grabbed a lap quilt and spread it across her lap. He smiled. "Is that better?"

She nodded and returned his smile.

"I told you I'd take care of you," he said with a wink.

Holly's breath hitched, leaving him wondering if he'd put his foot in his mouth one too many times.

CHAPTER SIX

By the time they reached the tree lot in town, Holly was shivering from the cold and wished she'd gone along with Ben in his buggy the way he'd asked her to instead of following him back to town in hers. She was excited to spend the morning with Ben, but even the giddiness she felt over that hadn't taken the chill out of her bones from the cold and lonely ride to town.

But if she'd gone with Ben in his buggy, there would have been too much explaining to do when her father saw them together, and her without her buggy. He would accuse her of trying to push her own agenda with Ben.

But what of it? Was it so wrong for her to want love instead of convenience? To not be a tradeoff for her father's debt? She supposed she owed him that much; after all, he'd cared for her during her whole life. But that was too high a price to pay—her gratitude in exchange for her happiness.

There had to be another way, but how could she go against her father without getting them both shunned? They'd met with Cousin Henry and Silas briefly after church services, and they'd not been the most patient of men. Holly had left their company at her father's request when Henry had begun to discuss money; now, she understood why she hadn't been a part of that conversation.

Was it possible that Ben's mother could be of some help to her?

Holly was desperately grasping for answers, but she was running out of time to change her future fate. According to her father, Silas would be coming by the bakery to take her for a buggy ride this very night.

She shivered. Not so much from the cold, but from the dread she felt deep in her heart.

She parked her buggy to the side of the lot, unable to keep her eyes off Ben, who tied her horse to the hitching post and then reached out his hand to help her down. Was he the answer to her prayers, or would she forever want what she could not have?

It seemed silly to long for a man who was right in front of her but was off-limits, unless she could find another way to compensate her cousin for the money her father owed, perhaps with a payment plan. That way, she would be free to do her own choosing for a husband.

Ben couldn't get rid of the weight that felt like an anvil resting on his shoulders. He almost wished his mother had not told him about Holly's betrothal to Silas. How could he stand by and watch Holly marry Silas Yoder? He was a harsh man—just like his father. They owned the largest dairy farm in the area, and he'd often tried to throw his weight around the community over the years because of it.

They'd squeezed out even the *English* competition, and because of it, most of the community depended on the Yoders for their milk, butter, and cheese. Ben and his family had become the exception since they kept goats for those needs, and that had always caused a rift between the families. Even though Henry Yoder's prices were far too high for his neighbors, he'd pushed his brother, who was the Bishop, to give him a large amount of control over the community.

Because of this, none dared to go against them to buy their meat or dairy needs from the local grocer. Instead, they paid the high prices the Yoders demanded. Over the years, they'd loaned money out to nearly every farm—except for Ben and his brothers, and most were indebted to them. Holly's father was now included. Henry used their money to get what he wanted, and it often hurt the members of the community, but Ben suspected he knew that.

Ben's father could not be bought by Henry Yoder, and because of it, there had been animosity between their families. When his father had passed away, Henry tried to come calling on Ben's mother, but he and his brothers would have no part in it.

They knew that Henry's main agenda was to control their tree farm like everything else in the community, and Ben had made an enemy of Silas when he'd stood up to Henry and driven him away from his mother.

In Ben's eyes, Silas and Henry were opportunists. He couldn't see Holly being happy with a man like that. She was sweet and gentle—quite the opposite of Silas. It made him cringe to think of the harsh way Silas might treat Holly. And it made him sick that the man couldn't be kind long enough to land himself a wife the normal way. He had to purchase one with his wealth from a vulnerable man and down on his luck.

Ben didn't completely blame Holly's father. Being new to the area, he probably didn't realize the kind of man he was dealing with, cousin or not. He was just a man desperate to get away from a farm that was weighing him down. When his cousin offered to help him out, it came with a stipulation, and her father likely didn't understand the magnitude of what he was getting himself or his daughter into by agreeing to such an arrangement. Many marriages were arranged in the community through family members, but this one had come with too high of a price. Because of her father's despair, they took advantage of him, so the blame fell solely on Henry and Silas.

Ben led Holly to the enclosure of the tree lot, where he unlatched the lock on the gate and swung it wide open, exposing the already cut trees to the cold. The canopy kept the snow out of the lot itself, but the parking area was deep with snow.

"I'm going to have to get this shoveled before we open for business," he said, looking out at the small parking area.

"I can help some," Holly offered.

Ben scoffed. "I can't ask you to do that!" he said. "That's *mann's* work!"

"I wasn't going to shovel it," she said with a giggle. "I was thinking more of using my hands to clear away the snow."

She held up her mittened hands and smiled.

"Your hands?" Ben asked. "I wouldn't let you clear the snow with—or without a shovel."

She giggled. "Let me show you!"

Ben watched Holly grab a handful of snow and begin to form it into a large ball and then rolled it in the snow a few more times, watching it grow as it gathered the snow along the ground.

He threw his head back and chuckled as she pushed the large snowball until it was so big she struggled to push it around any longer.

"Let me help you," he said, approaching her and giving the large ball of snow one final shove until it was up against the gate. "I get what you're doing; that's pretty smart!"

She giggled and then formed another ball of snow and began to push it along, not making the next one quite as large. When it got to be too big for her, Ben stepped in and rolled it toward the first snowball and hoisted it up so that it rested on top.

Ben stood back and surveyed their work so far. "I think he's in proportion, don't you?"

Holly giggled. "*Jah,* I haven't made a snowman since I was a little girl; I'm surprised I still know how."

Ben put up a hand to her. "I have just the thing that will make this better; you get to work on making his head, and I'll be right back."

Ben left her outside the gate while he went into the shop area to get a few things. When he returned, she'd managed to put the snowball head on the top of their snowman and was busy trimming twigs for his arms.

Ben held up his surprise for her. "I always keep carrots behind the counter for my horse, so I thought it would make a nice nose." In the other hand, he opened a red velvet bag and dumped out the contents into his hand. "We sell these novelty bags of coal to the *Englishers,* and I thought a couple of the pieces would look nice for eyes."

Holly giggled, and it warmed his heart.

"Let me help," she said, grabbing the round pieces of coal.

Ben worked the long carrot into the center of the head while Holly fashioned a couple of eyes with the larger pieces of coal and then formed a smile on him with the smaller pebble-sized pieces at the bottom of the red velvet sack.

Then they stood back to admire their handiwork. Ben put a hand to his chin and tipped his head sideways. "He needs something else."

He crossed the parking lot to where his buggy was and grabbed something, rushing back to Holly's side. Then he placed his black felt hat on his head.

"Don't you need that hat?" Holly asked. "It looks like a *gut* one for church-going."

Ben held it up and put his finger through the hole in the side. "One of the goats nipped it off my head one day and decided to chew a hole in it before I could get it away from him."

Holly giggled. "I would have liked to have seen that."

Ben chuckled. "I can see you have a warped sense of humor."

She held a hand up to her mouth and suppressed another giggle. "I'm sorry; I know I shouldn't laugh."

Ben chuckled. "*Nee,* you should laugh because it's funny. *Mei brudder,* Luke, didn't think it was very funny; it's his hat!"

Holly let her giggle escape her, and Ben threw his head back and laughed with her.

When they settled down, Ben looked around at the thin layer of snow that remained on the surface of the parking lot.

"That was a great idea you had to use the snow in the parking lot," Ben said. "Not only was it *gut* for packing, but now the snow isn't so deep, and the cars won't slide around or get stuck."

She held up her snowy mittens and smiled. "I told you I could clear your parking lot with only my hands."

He returned her smile. "You have a talent for making a chore like shoveling turn into a fun activity."

"And now you have a snowman to guard your lot," she said with a giggle. "Much like a scarecrow guards a field."

Ben put a hand to his chin. "What is he guarding against?"

"It isn't guarding against, but for," Holly said whimsically. "It attracts the Christmas spirit and keeps it from fading away before the snow melts."

"I like that!" Ben said. "But he's still missing something." He pulled off his red scarf and wrapped it around the snowman's neck and stood back to admire him once more.

"He's perfect!" Holly gushed.

"I was thinking the same thing about you," Ben said, feeling suddenly bold.

She smiled shyly. "It would be easy to return such a compliment."

Ben felt his heart skip a beat. Her comment gave him pause; was it possible she was willing to go against her father's arrangement for her and give him a chance? If only she knew how he felt about her. Maybe then there would be no question. But did he have the courage to come right out and tell her he wanted to court her?

Holly felt her cheeks warm up when Ben stood near her. Were they flirting? She was certain her father had spilled the news to Ben's mother while they were outside looking at the goats last night after supper. It wasn't like him to keep such a thing to himself.

Especially since he already suspected she had an interest in Ben. He would have made certain Ben's mother knew she was spoken for and would let her give him the news. That way, he would not have to be responsible if she should make a mistake and break her engagement with her foolish whims.

But was it really foolish to want love? She didn't believe so, and it seemed that either Ben didn't know of her engagement, or he was trying to ignore it the same as she was. Either way, she intended to explore that interest he seemed to have in her for all its worth. The only way she would get out of her commitment to Silas was if she had another offer, but what if Ben neglected to offer because he knew her secret?

Should she be honest and upfront with him about the engagement her father arranged on her behalf? If there was a way out of having to marry Silas, she prayed God would give her one

Holly followed Ben into the shop beside the canopy where they housed the trees. Twinkly white lights were strung all around, and red bows were scattered into every little nook. Then her eyes fixed on something she'd never seen before. So mesmerized by it, she closed the space between herself and the object as if somehow drawn to it. She reached out her hand and touched the ball of leafy greenery with the white and red berries. It was a handmade object of decoration, and its simplistic beauty puzzled her.

"It's mistletoe," Ben said, interrupting her whimsical thoughts.

"Mistletoe?" she repeated. "What is it used for?"

"The *Englishers* use it as a tradition at Christmastime; the legend supposedly says that if a woman is caught under the mistletoe, she must be kissed, and if she refuses, it's considered to be bad luck."

Holly giggled. "That's silly, but I like it."

"I'm glad to hear that," Ben said, pointing upward. "Because you're standing right under it, and it would be bad luck if you refused a kiss from me."

Holly's gaze followed his gesture to the ball of mistletoe hanging above her head from a velvety red ribbon. Her breath caught in her throat as Ben closed the space between them. Was this the answer to her prayers?

Her lashes fluttered. "I suppose in the name of luck I can hardly refuse," she said barely above a whisper.

Ben's lips covered hers in a simple, warm kiss that lingered only long enough to make her want more.

His lips were warm, and they tasted of fresh peppermint stick. She closed her eyes, wishing for another kiss, and he didn't disappoint her. When his lips made contact with hers again, she threw her arms around his neck, deepening the kiss.

He pulled her close to him using one hand around her waist, and then cupped her face with both hands, warming her cool cheeks, his kiss stirring a fire deep within her that made her feel warm all over.

Was she dreaming? If so, she didn't want to wake up for a long time.

CHAPTER SEVEN

When Holly and Ben had reached the bakery with all the things she had picked out—including the mistletoe, she was ready to get inside the warm bakery, but she wanted to help Ben bring in all the stuff.

Ben hopped down from his buggy and tide up Holly's horse after tying his. Then he reached up to help Holly down, his hand lingering on hers as she stood facing him, both smiling. Oh, how she wanted to kiss him, but she knew better than to risk being seen from the large window in the bakery where her father was most likely watching from the kitchen.

"Why don't you go inside, and I'll bring everything in," Ben said.

He winked at her, and she smiled before turning toward the bakery. Once inside, the aroma of fresh-baked bread brought a smiled to her lips

Her father was not in the kitchen as she'd expected him to be. She had to assume he was either running errands or had gone upstairs to nap while the bread cooled. Had she really been gone long enough for him to finish the morning bread?

Every loaf of bread was cooling on the racks, but nothing else had been done. It was a good thing for her that she'd already made the cookies and pies for the day. Seeing them in the display case now let her know that her father had been hard at work all morning. Everything was ready for the first customer of the day, but they still had an hour before they opened for business. That would give her just enough time to help Ben set up the tree and all the decorations.

She pulled off her coat and put on a fresh pot of coffee, and then thought to ask if Ben might prefer hot cocoa just as she did. He appeared in the doorway at that moment with a big box of the decorations she'd chosen from his lot. She giggled at the enormity of her greed.

"I think I might have gone a little overboard with the decorations," she said.

He smirked. *"Nee,* you can never have too many decorations for Christmas. In my opinion, more is always better!"

She smiled, thinking how refreshing it was that they shared the same opinion on the subject. Her father was comparable to an *English* Scrooge and didn't see a practical need for decorating at Christmas. Her mother always loved to spread greenery and spices around the house during the holiday season, and she feared the overabundance of cheer might just be her father's undoing.

Holly lifted her eyes heavenward and whispered a prayer that he would not make her put it all away. He'd not looked forward to Christmas the way she'd hoped he would. She'd only agreed to leave their farm to make him happy. She knew he couldn't bear to endure another Christmas there without her mother in their home.

They'd picked up and left the memories in Grabill, and Holly wanted nothing more for her father than for him to enjoy this Christmas, especially since it was quite possible it would be her last with him by herself. Though she did not want the marriage to Silas, another idea crept into her mind as she watched Ben unpack the many bows and strings of lights that she prayed would make her father's bakery the most inviting business on the block.

"Would you like some hot cocoa to warm you up?" she asked. "Or would you prefer *kaffi* instead?"

He looked up from his work and winked. "Surprise me!"

Holly felt her heart fluttering behind her ribs. Did that handsome man have any idea what he was doing to her heart? She had no defense against Cupid's arrows that Ben was shooting her direction every time he winked or smiled. But the kiss they shared had nearly caused her to pass out.

Then her thoughts shifted, causing her heart to slam against her ribs. Would Ben still be so eager to wink and smile and kiss her if he knew she was promised to another man?

Holly shook off the negative thoughts, determined to make the most of what little time she had with Ben. She wasn't about to spoil her chances at winning his heart with a melancholy mood. It was Christmastime, and she was ready to start cheering up the place with a little help from her handsome new friend.

Ben dragged in the tree with a bit of effort, and Holly rushed to close the door he'd propped open before too much snow blew inside the bakery. She shivered from the cold gust of wind, and before she knew it, Ben was at her side, pulling her into his arms.

"You're colder than I am," she giggled, pushing at him playfully.

He chuckled. "Why do you think I came over here? To get warm!"

"Hmm, charming and witty," she said. "I'm not so sure I can defend myself against such a strong temptation."

He waggled his eyebrows. "Then, I suppose all that's left to do is to give in to me!"

"Well, now you're taking all the fun out of it!" she said with a giggle.

"*Ach,* I think this could be very fun with you, but we don't have much time to get this tree up before you open for business," he reminded her.

She tipped her head and smiled. "I'll get you some cocoa to warm you up."

"*Danki,*" he said. "I'll have this tree up in no time at all. It's warm enough in here that the branches should drop fairly quickly so I can get the lights strung."

"How long do you think it will take?" she asked from the kitchen.

"Just long enough for us to tie the velvet bows for the tree," he answered, his back to her.

She paused at the counter, watching him work. He was strong, handling the large tree without help, but she supposed he was used to it. She felt a blush warm her cheeks, thinking about the strong muscles she could see beneath his button-up shirt. He'd shed his coat, probably too warm in the bakery. Her father had left the ovens on, likely thinking she'd be back in time to slip the premade batches of sugar cookies in before they opened.

With Ben preoccupied straightening the tree in the stand, she put in the first four trays and turned on the timer in case she got too distracted with Ben there. Besides, she would do well to keep herself busy in case her father came back from his errands. It wouldn't sit right with him if he caught them in an embrace. There would be plenty of time to tell her father she'd fallen for Ben and did not want to marry Silas. It would probably upset him, but she would work hard to repay the money her cousins loaned them.

Surely her father would understand and respect her feelings, wouldn't he?

Ben stole another glance in Holly's direction, making a note of the constant change in her expression. She seemed to be hard at work, trying to hide what was weighing on her mind. Was he the reason she appeared so distraught? She'd kissed him back like a woman in love, but was she torn about her marriage contract with Silas? If he had his way, he'd march right over to Silas's house and tell him Holly was *his* betrothed now, but he knew that wasn't true. He hadn't even taken her for a buggy ride yet.

Unless their first kiss counted as a promise between them, Ben might not have a leg to stand on when it came to claiming

Holly's heart. He'd fallen for her; there was no doubt about his feelings for her. That kiss was what did it for him. The minute his lips had touched hers, his heart belonged to her, whether she was ready for it or not.

He busied himself, setting the tree straight, hoping it would keep his mind off Holly long enough for him to think logically about his dilemma, but he was constantly aware of her near him. It made his heart beat out of control. He couldn't think past how much he cared for her already. The more he thought about the sickening offer Silas had made, the more anger rose from his gut.

What he couldn't figure out is why Holly hadn't said anything about it to him yet? What was she waiting for? What would he do if she never mentioned it? Should he bring it up? He blew out a breath.

Not a chance! I don't want to ruin whatever this is between us.

But what would happen to their budding relationship once Silas came to claim his bride? Would Ben have any claim on her other than the kiss they shared?

Once the tree was set in place, he went to work hanging the mistletoe near the tree, hoping Holly would stand under it again, and it would give him the chance to steal another kiss. Not that he'd had to steal the first one; she'd given herself freely to him. As if she longed to give her heart to someone other than Silas. His own mother had told him that Holly had rebelled against her father's arrangement with Silas. He prayed that meant there was room for him to stake a claim on her heart.

Even if she didn't marry him, Ben could not stand by and watch her marry Silas. Though he didn't know her very well yet, he knew she did not deserve to be stuck for the rest of her life with someone, so mean he would make her miserable.

But did Ben have the right to mess with her future? After all, Holly's father had put up the bakery as security for that arrangement, and the two would be left with nothing if Silas and his father called the loan to be paid before they'd made any profits. Bishop Yoder could not be counted on; he was just as corrupt as his brother. Many in the community had left because of the Bishop, and many more would if he continued to do his brother's bidding. Too many in their community had suffered because Bishop Yoder would not stand firm against Henry.

Could Ben stand up against him if it came to that? He was old enough to be on his own, but he didn't want to lose what he had with his brothers and their business. Besides, his mother still needed him and his brothers a great deal since his father's death. He knew his mother would urge him to follow his heart, but he was torn.

He pulled in a deep breath, thinking he was being foolish and overthinking the whole situation, but he had a bad habit of thinking too much sometimes.

Ben glanced at Holly once more, who was busy putting together a tray of refreshments for them. He hurried to fasten the mistletoe to the ceiling with some thin wire before she came over to investigate the job that he had done putting up the tree.

Right on cue, Holly emerged from the kitchen with the tray of hot cocoa and cookies, her green eyes sparkling when she saw the tree standing so majestically in the corner.

"It's absolutely delightful!" she said in a sing-song voice.

She set the tray down on the nearest table in the dining room and rushed to the tree, burying her face deep within its branches and breathing in, a smile so wide it brought a smile to Ben's face. She was so lovely to watch, her excitement about the tree catching her off-guard once more with the mistletoe.

Did he dare interrupt her reverie to point it out to her that she was once again standing beneath the mistletoe? He longed for another excuse to kiss her, and he might not get another chance if her father returned to the bakery anytime soon.

Ben cleared his throat and smiled when she turned to look at him. His gaze lifted, and hers followed.

"You did it to me again!" she said with a giggle.

"I think we should give this kissing thing another try," he suggested, trying to hide his smile. "To give the bakery *gut* luck, of course."

"I can't deny we need a bit of luck," she said, biting her bottom lip.

Her cheeks were a tint of pink that brought a smile to his lips, and he realized he was enjoying making her blush.

Closing the space between them, Ben pulled her into his arms with a gentle tug, capturing her lips with a level of confidence that he hoped would make her understand he wanted her to be his.

She pulled away from him slightly, her eyes cast to the floor.

He tucked a finger under her chin and urged her to look at him. "What is it?" he asked.

"I have something I better tell you before this goes any further," she said, her voice shaking.

"If it's about you and Silas," he said. "I already know."

Her breath hitched, but he pressed another kiss to her lips.

"I don't care about the business arrangement your *vadder* made with Silas and Henry Yoder unless you intend to go through with it and marry him."

She shook her head, tears welling up in her eyes. "*Nee,* I didn't know about the promise *mei vadder* made with our cousins until two days ago."

"You mean he didn't even ask if you wanted to marry Silas?"

Her eyes cast downward; she shook her head with a slow sadness that broke Ben's heart.

Unable to help himself, he pulled her into his arms and showered her cheeks and hair with kisses. "I'll help you out of it any way I can, but I have to know the terms of the agreement."

Holly paused to look at him, a hopeful smile across her full lips. Ben dipped his face and pressed his lips against hers once more, unable to quench the swell of love he felt for her.

"Get your hands and your lips off my betrothed!" a male voice barked behind them.

Holly became rigid in his arms, her hands covering her face. Ben knew that voice before he even turned around. It was Silas, and by the tone of his voice, Ben would have to guess he was looking for a fight.

Ben would be more than happy to give him that fight; he cared that much for Holly.

CHAPTER EIGHT

Ben paused before releasing Holly from his embrace. Silas had certainly spoiled the moment between them, but more than that, he was still laying claim on her.

"I'm sorry, Silas," Holly said with a shaky voice. "But, I'm Ben's betrothed, not yours!"

Ben felt his heart thump out of rhythm. He'd not asked her to marry him, not that he wouldn't and very soon, but he hadn't had the chance. Besides, it was too soon, wasn't it?

Ben peered into her green eyes, hoping for an explanation from her. She leaned in toward him and whispered close to his ear.

"Please go along with me," she begged. "I don't want to marry him."

That wasn't the explanation he was looking for or even wanted. He did want to marry her, but she'd crossed the finish line before he'd even begun the race.

He nodded methodically. How could he refuse her request, even if it was a request to *pretend* to be her betrothed? He didn't want to pretend; he wanted the real thing, but surely they weren't ready for that yet—which probably explained why she was making things up for the sake of getting rid of Silas. She'd used the kiss between them as her way out.

She hadn't even given him a chance. She could have said they were courting, but everyone in the community knew that meant marriage would eventually follow. Had she said it because she wanted to be betrothed to Ben? He guessed not since she begged him to go along with a lie.

Pain pierced his heart as he lifted his gaze toward Silas. The man was seething.

"I won't stand for this," he barked. "You were promised to me, and now you'll have to sell the bakery to pay off your *vadder's* debt. And I'm going to suggest that both of you be shunned for your behavior!"

With that, he left the bakery, leaving Ben to face the confusion between himself and Holly. He would do anything for her— even marry her if that was what she wanted, but the way she'd said it to Silas left him wondering if she'd used the kiss between them just to get herself out of the commitment her father had made on her behalf. He didn't want to be in the middle of this mess, but he'd helped to put them there.

"Do you think he's serious about getting us shunned?" Holly asked with a sniffle.

Ben grimaced. "*Jah,* he means it, and he'll probably succeed because his *onkel* is the Bishop."

She nodded. "I'm sorry; I didn't plan to tell Silas we were betrothed, but I panicked."

She looked so distraught; how could he not forgive her.

"It's alright," Ben said. "We'll figure this thing out. In the meantime, maybe I should go home and warn *mei familye.*"

She nodded. "*Jah,* of course."

"I can come back later to help you smooth things over with your *dat* if you need me to," he offered.

She shook her head and bit her bottom lip. "I got us into this mess; I better be the one to get us out."

She certainly was an independent sort of woman, wasn't she? Ben wasn't sure how he felt about that, but he supposed she was used to being tough on the exterior. He could clearly see she was falling apart on the inside. It made him want to draw her back into his arms, but he'd made a big enough mess of things already.

"I'm sorry if I got you into trouble," he said before turning to walk out the door.

She flashed him a weak smile. "I'm not."

He closed the space between them, unable to help himself. He wanted to claim her as his own.

Holly melted into Ben's broad frame, her quivering lips finding strength in his. Would he be able to forgive her for the way she'd pushed him into lying for her? She hadn't meant for it to come out, and maybe she'd overreacted when she'd looked into Silas's angry eyes.

"I didn't mean to get you mixed up with me and my problems," she said in between kisses.

He smiled. "Too late." He bent to kiss her again, and this time, it was her father who raised his voice from behind them.

"*Dochder,* what is the meaning of this?"

Holly straightened up, unable to look her father in the eye. She shook, but she felt Ben's steady hand grasp hers for strength.

"I can explain, Mr. Yoder," Ben said with a confidence that put Holly more at ease. "I've asked your *dochder* to marry me, and she has consented. With your permission, I'd like to come courting."

What was he saying? Was he trying to protect her from trouble with her father? He hadn't proposed to her.

"I forbid it!" he barked, his face twisted in anger. "You are already promised to Silas."

"You made that promise, *Dat,*" she declared. "I didn't promise him, and I don't want to marry him; I want to marry Ben."

She hadn't meant to say that last part; they hadn't even discussed anything about marriage. But still, her heart knew what it wanted, and that was not Silas.

"You know why that arrangement was made, and I forbid you to see Benjamin again," her father demanded.

Ben leaned toward her and whispered to her. "I better go; we can fix this later. If you need me, get word to me."

Holly nodded, and Ben's hand slipped from hers, leaving it cold and shaking.

Ben rushed home and went straight to his mother, pleading with her to help with Holly's father.

"Do you really want to marry Holly," his mother asked. "Or do you feel the need to rescue her from having to marry Silas Yoder? I know the two of you have been rivals for many years, and I want you to examine if your involvement is because of your feelings about Silas, or about your feelings for Holly."

Ben didn't have to think about it. He knew how he felt about her.

"I admit I have strong feelings against Silas, but that has nothing to with Holly," he said. "He won't be kind to her, I know that, but I care very much for her. We shared a kiss today—a couple of them. I know how I feel, and I want to marry her."

The excitement in his voice convinced his mother, but would his enthusiasm be enough to convince his brothers to help him?

Holly felt her heart thump an extra beat when the bell on the door to the bakery jingled, and in walked Ben's mother. She put on her best smile and greeted the woman.

"It's *gut* to see you," Holly said with a shaky voice.

"No need to be nervous," the woman leaned in and whispered. "I'm here to see your *vadder.*"

Holly fixed her eyes toward the kitchen behind her. "He's bringing out the trays of muffins to bake; I'll let him know you're here."

She went to the back and poked her head in the walk-in. "You have a guest in the dining room."

He looked up from sorting pies and cakes. "I'm in the middle of something. Who is it?"

"*Frau* Bontrager," Holly answered, not expecting her father's eyes to light up the way they did.

He half smiled and then checked himself under the scrutinizing stare from his daughter. "Tell her I'll be out there shortly; will you make ready some *kaffi* and a few sweets and ask her to take a seat in the dining room?"

Holly nodded, feeling a sense of shock at her father's sudden mood change. Was this the miracle she'd been praying for ever since Ben left the bakery this morning?

Whatever was going on, her father had acted like a whole different person just now, and it would seem he was sweet on Ben's mother, and that could be to her advantage.

"What do I have to do to convince you to help me?" Ben was practically begging Luke, but he was feeling mighty desperate.

"I need time to think about that," Luke said, running a hand through his thick hair. He replaced his black, Sunday hat on his head and put a hand to his chin as if he were deep in thought.

"I'm willing to put up my land as security," Ben begged.

He didn't care how desperate he sounded; he was indeed desperate to claim Holly and keep her from being forced to marry Silas.

Luke nodded. "Your land is adjoining mine, and that would be convenient for me."

"I plan on paying you back every penny, so you won't need to commandeer my land!"

"That's a lot of money," Luke reminded him. "And besides, what do you have left to offer them as security?"

"I was hoping I wouldn't need to offer my own *brudders* security," Ben fumed.

"You're asking each of us to give up our entire years' wages, and you won't even tell me why!" Luke barked.

"I want to marry Holly Yoder, and her father made a business deal and promised she would marry Silas Yoder in exchange for five thousand dollars to help him with unexpected expenses at the bakery," Ben said without taking a breath.

Luke smirked. "Knowing that bit of information, I'll gladly give up my wages, and I'd be willing to bet Simon will agree."

"Danki," Ben said. "This means a lot to me."

"Half the community is indebted to Silas and Henry Yoder," Luke said. "It's about time someone stood up to them."

"Silas came into the bakery this morning after Holly, and I brought the tree there, and he caught us kissing under the mistletoe."

Luke smiled and punched his brother in the arm playfully. "You kissed her? What was it like?"

Ben sighed. "It was wonderful, except that Silas wrecked it by threatening to have the Bishop shun us."

Luke raised his eyebrows. "Do you think he's serious?"

Ben let go of a short bark of laughter, surprised at his brother's lack of urgency for the situation. "Of course, he's serious. I think we need to vote the Bishop out and get someone appointed who won't turn his back on all the corruption Henry and Silas have been involved with the past ten years or so."

"I think they started causing trouble right about the time Henry became a widower."

"We know firsthand how painful it can be to lose a parent, but it didn't corrupt us the way it did Silas," Ben admitted.

"That's because we have bigger hearts, I guess," Luke said with a chuckle.

"Maybe we need to just pray more for him; you know the Bible tells us to pray for our enemies and those who persecute us," Ben reminded his brother.

"That isn't always easy to do, but you're right," Luke agreed.

"Let's see what we can do about getting that money to Mr. Yoder before it's too late," Ben said. "Maybe if we head off the trouble with Silas, he'll be so happy to have his money that he won't push the issue with Holly."

"I pray this works for you, little *brudder!*" Luke said.

For the first time in his life, it hadn't bothered him that Luke referred to him as his *little brother.* Was it possible that meant he was growing up?

Ben waited for his mother to return from her visit with Holly's father in town. She'd offered to talk to him, hoping she could somehow cushion the tension between the families. If he knew his mother, she would also work her magic to make way for him to marry Holly. She had a gentle way of persuasion in her soft heart that had always worked on his father. Surely, it would work on Mr. Yoder too; after all, he was a man who seemed to take an interest in his mother and was likely not immune to her feminine charm.

Armed with a pocketful of money, thanks to the generosity of his brothers, Ben was confident between his mother's words and paying off Mr. Yoder's debt, they could somehow fix this.

When his mother's buggy came up the driveway, Ben went out to unhitch her horse for her. He tried to gauge how the meeting had gone by his mother's expression, but he could see she'd pasted on a smile.

His shoulders dropped. "You didn't have any luck, did you?" he asked.

She shrugged after he helped her out of the buggy. "It wasn't hopeless, but he did tell me the only way he could break the contract was if he lost the bakery to Silas and Henry, or if he was able to pay back the loan, which he can't because they haven't had a chance to make a profit yet."

Ben reached into his pocket and pulled out the wad of money and showed his mother.

"Where did you get all that money?" she asked, her eyes wide.

"From my generous *brudders!*" Ben said with a smile. "We've had an exceptional year with the trees so far, and it looks even more promising. I can give it to Mr. Yoder, and then he won't have to give up his *dochder* to Silas."

"Aren't you afraid of hurting the man's pride," his mother asked.

Ben let out a heavy sigh. *"Jah,* it crossed my mind that he might be too prideful to even accept it, and that's why I've decided to offer it as a bride price—the same way Silas did."

"Aren't you afraid of insulting Holly with that kind of offer?"

Ben kicked at the snow. "*Mamm,* don't make me think too much about this. I've made up my mind; pray that it won't backfire in my face."

She pulled her son into a warm hug. "I will do that for you."

Ben assisted his mother in the house since she was still favoring her swollen ankle. "You've already done far more than I could ask for, and I'm grateful for you, *Mamm.*"

She turned to smile at him before walking into the house. "I planted the seed, now it's up to *Gott* to grow the tree."

He kissed his mother on the cheek and hurried to get her buggy horse put away. He couldn't wait to go to Holly's father and ask his permission to marry his daughter.

CHAPTER NINE

Ben arrived at the bakery full of nervous energy, but eager to hand over the bride price for Holly's hand in marriage. Normally, such an extravagant amount would not be offered as an engagement gift, but he was desperate to save her from Silas and would have come up with more money if necessary.

It wasn't so much that he worried Holly would reject him, but that her father would continue block in his plan to marry her. His mother had admitted Ben might have a tough time convincing the man to trust him over his own family. But she had done her best to soften the man's heart. Now it was up to Ben to go the distance. The last thing he wanted was to start off on the wrong footing with his would-be father-in-law.

Pulling in a deep breath, Ben entered the bakery, the warm cinnamon aroma coming from the kitchen, making his mouth water.

Ben spotted Holly right away. If not for the jingling bell on the door giving him away, she would not have looked up, but the smile she greeted him with warmed his heart after the cold buggy ride into town.

He nodded and returned her smile, thinking he could get used to seeing the welcoming beauty of her smile every day for the rest of his life.

Stomping his boots on the rug just inside the door so he wouldn't track slush onto the tile floor, Ben couldn't take his eyes off Holly while she dried her hands on her apron and moved toward the front counter.

He cleared his throat as he approached the counter where Holly met him with a cup of steaming coffee, a muffin, and her brilliant smile.

"You look cold," she remarked as she pushed the coffee toward him.

"Danki."

Ben gave a little shiver as he pulled off his gloves. "The temperature has dropped considerably since those clouds rolled in. I expect it'll be snowing pretty heavy by the time we open the tree lot this afternoon."

"Your *mudder* was here a little while ago," Holly mentioned. "It was *gut* to see her, but she was visiting *mei dat.*"

She flashed him a smile that showed she misunderstood his mother's visit to the bakery to talk with her father, and Ben figured he better set her straight before she got her hopes up for the two of them making a match. Ben knew his mother would never consider a courting relationship with a man who was so seemingly mixed up as Holly's father. His mother didn't approve of how he was handling his daughter's affairs, and despite any possible interest she might have in the man, she would wait to see how things panned out from here.

Ben cleared his throat again and took a sip of his coffee. "I'm here to see your *vadder,* too."

"He's upstairs taking a nap," she said quietly, glancing at the clock on the wall. "Do you have time to wait? He should be up shortly."

Ben was ready to get his talk with the man over with, but he would much rather spend some time with Holly.

"I can stay," he said. "As long as you'll join me with a cup of *kaffi.*"

She let her gaze fall over the three customers in her dining room and then nodded. "Why don't we sit by the tree; I'll grab a cup and be right with you."

Ben hadn't noticed the tree until she'd pointed it out. He'd had his focus so trained on her when he'd entered the bakery, he completely missed seeing the twelve-foot beauty.

"It looks *gut,*" he said as he crossed to where it filled the entire corner.

"*Danki,*" she said from the counter.

He went over and dipped his nose close to the branches and breathed in. She'd done a fine job of making all the bows from the spools of red, velvet ribbon he'd given her from the tree lot. A primitive angel made from dried twigs sat majestically at the treetop, and Ben was fascinated by its structure.

Holly came up behind him just then. "*Mei mudder* made that for our fireplace mantel when I was just a little girl," she said thoughtfully, relishing the memory.

"It makes the tree," Ben said with a smile.

"*Mei dat* doesn't like the tree," she said as she sat across from him at the small table in the corner. "He thinks it is too *English,* but as you can see, I have a few customers. They've been coming in slowly throughout the day."

"I'm happy for you," he said.

"The lovely wreath you made and hung on the door brings them in," she said, sipping her coffee.

"The nativity scene in the window display is an eye-catcher too," he said.

"*Dat* made that for *mamm*," she said. "We don't have enough room in the loft upstairs to put such things, and I thought it would be a shame to leave them boxed up because *mei dat* doesn't want to face them. It wasn't my intention to hurt him, but he took it that way."

Ben reached a hand across the table and covered her hand with his. The warmth of it made his heart flutter. "*Mei brudders* and I have gone through the same things trying to shelter *mei mamm* from memories of *mei dat* that might upset her, but we can't shelter them from reality. They're widowed, and that is their lives, but they don't have to stay alone for the rest of their lives. I believe *mei mudder* has an interest in your *dat,* and I believe they could be happy together, but they have to move beyond the hurts of the past and live for their future. It isn't *gut* to grieve forever."

"I agree," she said.

"I also know *mei mamm* well enough to know that she won't stand by and let you marry Silas when her own son is in love with you and wants to marry you," Ben said.

Holly's breath hitched. "You *love* me?"

Ben stood and reached out his hand and pulled her under the mistletoe. When his lips met with hers, he didn't care how many were watching until the stern voice of her father thundered from behind them.

"Holly, I thought you understood I've forbidden you to see Ben," he hollered. "Why have you rebelled against me? This *mann* is not your betrothed, yet I find you a second time mixed up in a romantic and forbidden embrace with him."

"Mr. Yoder," Ben said, letting Holly slip from his arms. "I brought you the money to pay back your cousin; I've brought it as an engagement gift for Holly's hand in marriage."

"I forbid it!" Holly's father said, turning his back to them. "Tell your *mudder* I'm sorry, but I just can't approve the marriage."

Ben looked at Holly, her red-rimmed green eyes made him want to scoop her up and run off with her, but he knew that wouldn't solve anything. The only thing he knew to do was to plead with Silas and Henry. But first, he would go to the Bishop.

"I'll go, but I'm not giving up on Holly," Ben said, flashing her an apologetic look. "I have the money to repay your debt."

With that, he left the bakery, his stomach in knots. He didn't really believe that her father opposed their marriage since he had the money to get him out of debt, but he supposed there was a tie stronger than that debt that bound him. Henry Yoder had a way of reducing a man down to nothing with his personal loans, but he never thought the man would sink so low as to buy his son a bride with his greed.

Holly let go of the sobs that choked her the minute Ben walked out of the bakery.

"Dat," she sobbed. "How could you turn him down?"

"Because we are indebted to Henry for that money, and you know he will never let us out of that debt without you marrying Silas," he grumbled.

"But *Dat,* I don't want to marry him; I don't love him," she cried. "I love Ben, and I don't understand why you thought you needed to *buy* me a husband."

"It didn't start out that way," he said, hanging his head. "I'm ashamed to admit that I needed to get away from the memories of your *mudder* so badly that Henry was able to take advantage of my desperation, and I'm sorry."

"I want the kind of love you had with *mamm,"* she said, her lower lip quivering. "I know I haven't known Ben very long, but you and *mamm* had the kind of love the Bible talks about how a *mann* is to love his *fraa* as Christ loved the church. Do you really think a selfish *mann* like Silas, who would stoop to using threats and blackmail to get himself a bride, could love me that way?"

"But your *mudder* was bought for me with a milk cow!" he said.

Holly's eyes bulged as she pulled in a gasp. "You don't mean that! *Mamm* loved you, and I know you loved her too!"

"Of course, I loved her," he said. "But her *familye* was very poor, and *mei vadder* had a little more than they did; he knew that I was in love with her, but I didn't think she liked me, so he offered her *vadder* the milk cow as an engagement gift, and he took it. Later, I discovered that she had a secret crush on me all along and was too shy to act on it, but the cow had already been exchanged."

"*Dat,* I had no idea," she said.

"Her *familye* needed that cow because they were very poor, and I wanted to marry your *mudder,* so I thought it was the perfect solution to everyone's problem. I suppose I was thinking the same way with you and the bakery. But now I realize it's not the same because you and Silas don't even know each other, and you don't have any affection for him. Will you forgive me?"

"Of course, I forgive you, *Dat,*" she said, sniffing back tears. "But how are we going to get out of this mess with Silas? He's expecting me to marry him, and I can't do it—not even for the sake of the bakery. I hope you understand."

Her father let out a long sigh. "*Jah,* I understand, but we might lose the backing of the entire community. With his *brudder* as the Bishop, Henry has no reason to let us out of that contract with him. He could have us shunned."

"If I know Ben, he's probably on his way to the Bishop now to make Henry take that money because I won't be able to marry Ben if we get shunned."

"I'm sorry I got us into this mess," her father said. "I wasn't thinking about how this would affect you."

"It didn't help things with *Frau* Bontrager," she said boldly. "I've seen the way the two of you still desire a relationship like that. I don't want this debt to ruin both our chances at a happy future."

"You're right about that," her father said. "I've been as *narrish* as a *vadder* could be. I suppose if we have to, we can give up the bakery to keep from being shunned, but that means we will have to start over again."

Holly smiled. "I have a feeling Ben's *familye* would help to care for us."

"Let's hope it doesn't come to that," her father said, patting her hand.

Holly knew her father loved her, but his grief had left him a little bit misguided in thinking. If they were to get out of this without any more grief, she would have to be a part of the decision-making from this point on. "I think that if Cousin Henry accepts Ben's money for your debt, you should offer his *familye* a partnership with the bakery since they gave up their entire year's salary to loan you that money," Holly said gently.

Her father nodded. "I agree, but I'd like to do better than that; I'd like to marry the Widow Bontrager and take care of her. That way, Ben will be free to take care of *mei dochder,"* he declared with a gentle smile.

Holly threw her arms around her father and sobbed, but this time, they were happy tears.

CHAPTER TEN

Ben arrived at the Bishop's house just in time to run into Silas and Henry. His timing had been both a blessing and a curse. But at least this way, he could accomplish two tasks in one. At least he prayed it would happen that easily. The only problem he could see at this point was that they'd had a chance to present their arguments to the Bishop before he could. That was two strikes against him since their family relation counted for a lot more than opinion or even what might be morally right in this situation.

Ben shook off the negative feelings and went to the door where he was welcomed as if he'd been expected.

And why wouldn't he be? He was likely the reason for Henry's visit.

Inside the kitchen, *Frau* Yoder was abuzz at the stove, pouring another cup of coffee for their newest guest. He thanked her when she handed it to him and then sat with the others, his heart pumping so hard it was making him shake. He took in a deep breath and tried to calm himself.

"I'm glad you showed up here," the Bishop said. "It saves me a trip out to your farm."

Ben raised an eyebrow. "*Jah?*" he questioned the man.

The Bishop wrapped his hands around his coffee mug and darted his gaze between his brother and his nephew. "Henry tells me that Silas caught you in an intimate embrace with his betrothed. Is this true?"

Ben nodded slowly as he reached into his coat pocket and pulled out a thick stack of bills. He slid the money across the table toward Henry. "I've come to pay off the debt for the bakery and to ask for the release of the contract for Holly's hand."

Henry's face twisted with anger as he shoved the stack of bills back toward Ben, scattering the money across the table. "That isn't enough to cover the debt!" his voice thundered in the small kitchen.

Ben stiffened. "All five thousand—count it."

Henry leered at Ben. "I don't need to count it; five thousand doesn't even begin to cover the interest for the loan I gave him, and the terms haven't been met. I intend to see my son marry that girl."

Ben held his ground despite the rattling he felt deep in his gut. "How much more do you need to let her out of that contract?"

"I want your land!" Henry said, leaping from his chair and letting it scrape against the floor behind him. It teetered for a moment and then fell back with a crash.

Ben jumped, but righted himself quickly, hoping Henry hadn't noticed he'd rattled him to his very core. He couldn't give up his land. Talking to this man was worse than dealing with a spoiled child who believed throwing tantrums would get him what he wanted.

"You've always been after our land, and you won't get your greedy hands on it even if I have to face shunning to keep it!" Ben said, raising his voice. "But I'm going to talk to everyone in the community who owes you money or who have had their land stolen by you, and I'm going to get up a petition to have you shunned and your *brudder* removed as Bishop!" Ben glared at the Bishop, who had always looked the other way when his brother had behaved badly to let him know that this time he was not going to get away with it.

"Now let's not get hasty," the Bishop tried to say.

Ben snatched his money from the table and excused himself from the meeting, shouldering out into the cold and blizzardy afternoon. He'd made the threat, and now he would have to follow through and hope he could gain some support from the members of his community. It would not be an easy task, but it was better than standing by and allowing another injustice by Henry, especially since it involved the woman he wanted to spend the rest of his life with.

Knowing his work was cut out for him today, he needed to see as many in the community as possible. His best bet to try to thwart Henry's plans was to attend the meeting at the church this evening. If he could get enough cooperation from people in the community, he could present his argument there. It was the perfect place to handle his business; by interrupting a meeting intended to aid the very same families that Henry had devastated with his greed. Most of them would back him since he was sure they were tired of depending on a struggling community to help them through another winter—especially when it was the head of that very community who was responsible for their poverty in the first place.

Warning them ahead of the meeting was crucial to Ben's plan. If he could get them geared up to fight at that meeting for their rights, then perhaps his own battle might also be won in the process.

When he returned home to gather his brothers for support, he was surprised to see

Holly's buggy in the driveway—or rather, her father's. His heart pounded at the thought of Mr. Yoder being there. Would he issue Ben a warning to stay away from Holly, or had he changed his mind about accepting the money? Either way, it was too late; Henry was not backing down from the debt owed to him. He wanted more money than was originally agreed upon, and he wanted Holly married to Silas, and nothing short of those two things would satisfy his greedy heart.

Luke met him in the driveway. "I'll put up your horse," he said, tipping his head toward the house. "You have guests waiting for you."

Guests? If they were both there, the news couldn't be all that bad, could it? Surely, he'd have made Holly stay at the bakery if it was bad news since he'd forbidden Ben to see her again.

Lord, give me the strength and courage to fix this. You know my heart, Lord; you know I love Holly. Please make a way for me to marry her if it's your will. Amen.

Ben took in a deep breath of icy air before entering through the kitchen door. The aroma of coffee and cinnamon bread filled him as he breathed in the warm air inside the house. He shrugged out of his snowy jacket and toed out of his slushy boots, leaving them by the door in the mudroom. Tiptoeing into the kitchen in his stocking feet, Ben weighed the mood in the room before pushing his way through the doorway. His gaze caught Holly's immediately, and she greeted him with a smile. That was a good sign, wasn't it?

Removing his hat and hanging it on the back of his chair, he sat across from Holly, trying not to become too presumptuous about the visit.

"I came here to apologize," Mr. Yoder spoke up.

Ben pointed toward himself and raised his eyebrows. "To me?"

Mr. Yoder nodded, covered *Frau* Bontrager's hand, and smiled at her.

What was going on here?

He looked to Holly for answers, and her smile gave it away. His heart did a flip behind his ribs.

"You mean you'll accept the engagement gift I've offered you for Holly?"

He shook his head. "I went to the bank next door to the bakery and told them of my dilemma, and they assured me that my cousin's contract would not hold up in court for Holly's hand, but that they could call the loan and take the bakery. But the bank also agreed to give me a small business loan for the five thousand and pay him back so we could keep the bakery."

His mother smiled at him. "Even if we get shunned, I want you to know that we won't stand in the way of your plans with Holly."

She clenched Mr. Yoder's hand, and Ben understood. He pulled his mother into a hug; he was happy for her. He was happy for himself too, but mostly, he was happy for his mother and Holly's father that they'd worked everything out.

Ben sat back down and steepled his hands in front of him, turning his gaze on Holly only for a minute before addressing her father. "We still have to give the community a chance to back us up. Will you go with me to visit our neighbors to see if we can get them to vote the Bishop out?"

"That's risky," Mr. Yoder said.

Ben held up a hand. "I'm sorry; I shouldn't have asked you to go against your *familye*."

Mr. Yoder chuckled. "That's not what I have a problem with. From what I hear, most of the community owes Henry money, and they are all terrified he will make an example of them the way he has to some of the others, and winter is a bad time for them to become homeless. Are we prepared to offer them shelter if they stand with us against Henry and the Bishop?"

Ben let out a long sigh. "I hadn't thought about that, but I do believe we should attend that meeting tonight at the church. It might be that *Gott* would open a door for us."

"If nothing else, it will give the Bishop the chance to shun us publicly," his mother said.

He hated that she was willing to be shunned for his happiness, but he suspected her future with Holly's father had added weight to her decision. He wondered what his brothers thought about the possibility of being shunned, but he supposed they would all work together as a family, and they would make it without the community if need be.

Ben reached for Holly's hand and led her out of the house and into the snowy afternoon. When they reached the paddock where his brother's horses were circling the pen, he stopped and faced her. "I suppose I should officially ask you to marry me," he said, casting his eyes out toward the horses.

"And I suppose I might have to say yes!" Holly said.

Ben chuckled. "Will you really? Will you marry me?"

She nodded, snowflakes weighing on her long brown lashes. She blinked them away, and Ben gazed dreamily into her spirited green eyes. It was there that he saw his future.

Bishop Yoder called the meeting to begin, and Ben, who sat in the row directly behind Henry and Silas, felt his heart trying to leap from his ribcage.

"Before we begin to discuss the progress we're making with the Christmas dinner for the less fortunate in our community, it is those members that I want to address more profoundly." Bishop Yoder paused and then cleared his throat before continuing. "My eyes have been opened to sin in our community—sin that I have allowed and even been guilty of participating in."

A few gasps erupted from the people assembled there, followed by a gentle hum of conversation among the crowd.

Bishop Yoder held up his hands to hush them. "Let me explain," he pleaded. "It seems that I'm faced with stepping down from my position as your Bishop if I continue to allow my own *brudder* to leach this community of its livelihood."

Henry jumped from his place in the front row and twisted his face in anger.

"What is this all about?" he shouted at his brother.

The Bishop lowered his head and shook it with shame. "How soon you forget, Henry, that it was I who gave you our *familye* farm when you married Ada. I was the eldest and the rightful heir of that land, and I gifted it to you out of love. Now you have used that land to gain more from some of our neighbors surrounding that farm when they could not pay back the money they owed you. In the past ten years since I've been the Bishop, I've looked the other way every time you've treated one of the members of our community unfairly. The people here don't respect either of us, and they don't care for us—they fear us—mostly you, and I won't stand by and watch you destroy our newest members—our own cousins!"

"I earned everything I have!" Henry shouted back at him.

His Bishop-brother held up his hands to stop Henry. "Except the *familye* farm, which I will take back from you unless you forgive the debt this community owes you!"

"You can't do that to me after I've built that farm to more than four times what it was when you gave it to me," Henry hollered.

"I can, and I will!" Bishop said, standing his ground. "I gave that land to you as a wedding gift, and after Ada died, you began to take it out on me and the entire community. Her death was an accident, and you need to stop trying to find blame in everyone here."

Henry held his fist in the air and shook it toward his brother. "They all stood by and watched her suffer and didn't lift a hand to help her! They let her die."

His voice broke on that last word, and there was silence in the church.

"That's not true, Henry," Bishop said with a quiet, gentle tone. "Everyone tried to help, but none of us knew she was allergic to bees. There were just too many stings, and they'd swarmed her when she knocked into that nest under the tree. No one had noticed the nest that day when they'd set up for the church picnic. It was an accident, and many of us got stung several times trying to get the nest and the swarm away from her, but it was her allergic reaction that caused her death—not any one of us here in this community. By the time we reached her, she was already dying, and there was nothing anyone could have done to save her."

"That's not true!" Henry shouted, dropping to his knees and sobbing. "Every one of you stood back and watched my Ada die."

Henry had been down by the creek, drawing water for the horses when it happened and had not gotten to her until it was too late. If only he'd been able to say goodbye to her, he might have had some sort of closure, but he'd been robbed of that.

Bishop Yoder left the front of the assembly and went to his brother to calm his much-needed sobs. The man hadn't shed a tear since his wife's death that anyone had seen. He'd become cold and bitter, and so full of anger that he'd made the entire community suffer from his grieving.

"You must forgive and come to terms with her death, or you will never be able to move on with your life," the Bishop warned his brother. "Let it go."

The wind blew through the rafters of the old barn that they used as a church building, causing Ben to shiver. The barn used to belong to Henry's family, but the Bishop had requested it be donated as the church building when he'd taken over as Bishop. Henry had reluctantly agreed to donate it despite the fact he'd built two more modern barns since then.

Ben wondered if the Bishop regretted spoiling Henry after he'd taken over his care when they were young. Samuel had been only eighteen years old when their parents had passed away, and he'd had to take over the care of ten-year-old Henry, who had been a surprise to his parents. They had been told they couldn't have any more children after Samuel, and so they'd begun the spoiling of Henry. Samuel had only furthered that when he'd taken over as caregiver for his brother at such a young age.

The barn remained quiet except for the gentle sobbing of Henry and the whistling of the wind coming in through the rafters of the barn. Ben had become restless after several minutes and decided to pray for the man. After all, the Bible urges us to pray for our enemies. Before long, Luke nudged him and leaned in to whisper in his ear.

"What do you think the chances are we might get our tree money back from you?"

Ben smirked at him and then shrugged.

"I don't know; the Bishop asked him to forgive all the debt, but I'm not sure he'll be willing."

Silas turned around in his seat and glared at Ben. Simon poked his ribs from the other side of him.

"What?" he whispered to his younger brother.

"Have some respect." He'd mouthed the words, but Ben understood.

Simon was right in reprimanding his older brothers. Ben motioned with a flip of his head toward the door, and they filed out of the row and out into the cold December air.

Ben picked up a forkful of ham and looked around the supper table at his family, including the newest member, his new stepfather, and soon-to-be father-in-law. That would take a lot of getting used to, but he would enjoy Sunday suppers with his family.

Holly's father had moved into the main house with his mother directly after the wedding, while Holly remained at the bakery. With his mother's ankle healed, she had begun to work with her husband at the bakery to give Holly a little free time to begin planning their wedding. Being older, Ben's mother and Holly's father had opted for an impromptu wedding the day following Henry's full confession in front of the community. He'd forgiven everyone's debt, including that which was owed for Silas, allowing Ben to marry Holly. He'd been able to give his brothers back the money they'd put up for security for the bakery, and Samuel had not needed to get a loan from the bank after all.

It had been an amazing turn of events that had started with the sobs of a grieving man and ended with a happy community.

For now, Ben would never take anything for granted again. Life was too short to hold onto past hurts and too short to hold grudges. Their community had already begun to mend this past week, and change had turned out to be a good thing for all of them.

Ben folded his napkin and tossed it onto his empty plate and then leaned back and rubbed his belly and smiled. If his mother and betrothed were going to cook like this every week, he was going to have to do a few more laps around the tree farm every day just to keep in shape.

"I hope you saved room for the apple pie I baked," Holly said with a giggle.

Ben groaned. "Can we go outside and work off some of that supper first?"

Ben's mother gave her a nod. "You go ahead; I'll start the dishes. That snow is for young people. I'd rather stay in here where it's warm and work on the supper dishes."

Holly smiled. *"Danki."*

Ben extended his hand to Holly, and they went outside where the late afternoon sun was just beginning to sink over the snowy horizon. Wispy flakes danced in the air around them

Holly reached down and picked up a handful of snow and tossed it playfully toward Ben. She winged him with the snowball, causing him to stoop to get a handful for himself.

Holly squealed and tried to get away, but she felt the spray of snow against her back. She laughed and rolled onto the snowy ground, her cable knit leggings covered in snow. "I give up!" she said with a giggle.

Ben collapsed to the ground with a chuckle. "That was too easy!"

Holly scooped a loose handful of snow and covered him with it, scrambling to her feet and squealing as he jumped up to go after her. He caught her in his embrace and kissed her cold, giggling lips, thankful he no longer needed mistletoe to give him the courage to kiss her.

"Let's go inside with the old folks and have some hot cocoa," he said with a chuckle. "It's too cold out here."

"Okay, but if you're not careful, you're going to start sounding like *mei dat!*"

Holly giggled, and Ben kissed her once again. "I'll gladly stay out here, but you're going to have a full-time job of keeping my lips warm."

Holly smiled. "I don't have a problem with that." She deepened the kiss, and they stayed out there until the sun went down.

Ben was all too happy to go inside though he'd have been content to stay out there in the cold and kiss her for longer, but there would be plenty of buggy rides in their future, and he had the rest of his life to kiss her, thanks to Henry's forgiving heart.

EPILOGUE

Silas stood between the trees watching the exchange between Holly and Ben, longing for such an easy relationship. He knew deep down it would have never worked out between him and Holly because he was just too awkward when it came to relationships with others. He had no friends; he didn't stand a chance since most of his peers came from the families his father had intimidated. Why would he think he could get a woman like Holly to love him just because his father paid for her? He hadn't been able to buy him any friends.

It saddened him that the only way he could get a bride was to have his father pay for one. But now that his father had made some positive changes, maybe it was time Silas made some too. But how? Where would he start?

He'd come over here to apologize, but now that he'd seen them together and how happy they were, he didn't dare to approach them. Would they even welcome him into their circle of friends and family? Though distant, he and Holly were family, and he prayed that might make a difference to her.

He leaned up against the tree, watching his cousin and her betrothed frolicking in the snow. They were happy—truly happy. The way his parents had been before his mother died. He missed his mother probably as much as his father did, but his *onkel* Samuel was right; it was time for them to put the past behind them. Not to be forgotten, but so they could heal the wounds that had nearly ripped the community apart.

Silas shivered and pulled his collar tighter to shelter himself from the frigid wind. What in the world was he doing out here in this weather not fit for man or beast? He let out a sigh, knowing he just couldn't help himself. He didn't have the guts to approach Holly and Ben yet, but he couldn't stop watching the happy couple with a saddened sense of envy. He longed for a relationship with a woman he didn't have to coerce into marriage.

With his father's new standing in the community, Silas had already decided he needed to make some changes too. He'd learned of a new family who'd just gotten settled into the community who planned to raise a small herd of cattle. Though they wouldn't directly compete with his father's dairy and beef business if they were small enough, Silas wondered how his father would handle a little competition. Only time would tell if his father's changes would stick.

Nonetheless, Silas felt compelled to reach out to the new family and help them get set up. They'd asked around for hired help, and Silas knew he was the man for the job. Besides, he needed to put a little distance between himself and his father's spoils. It was the only way he would ever be able to stand on his own as a man. He knew all there was to know about the cattle business thanks to his father, and he didn't need to work for a living, but if he was going to carve out a living on his own, he would never get a better opportunity to learn than to work for someone else. After all, he had plans to have his own cattle ranch one day.

If he was lucky enough to find love.

Silas let out a heavy sigh. Even if he did find someone, he had no idea how to go about courting a woman. His gaze turned back to Ben and Holly, who were laughing so hard it brought up a chuckle in Silas he had no idea where it had come from.

Was it possible he could learn something from the two of them? Only time and kindness on his part would mend those fences, but he was determined to try.

THE END

Printed in Great Britain
by Amazon